TOO GOOD TO BE TRUE

By KYLE HUNT

KILL A WICKED MAN
KILL MY LOVE
KILL ONCE, KILL TWICE
CUNNING AS A FOX
WICKED AS THE DEVIL
SLY AS A SERPENT
CRUEL AS A CAT
TOO GOOD TO BE TRUE

TOO GOOD TO BE TRUE

by Kyle Hunt

A COCK ROBIN
MYSTERY

THE MACMILLAN COMPANY

Library of Congress Catalog Card Number: 71-85123

First Printing

The Macmillan Company
866 Third Avenue, New York, N. Y. 10022
Collier-Macmillan Canada Ltd., Toronto, Canada

Printed in the United States of America

CONTENTS

CHAPTER

1	"The Trouble with You . . ."	7
2	"The Trouble with Me . . ."	16
3	Sent with Malice	24
4	Denial	33
5	Charlotte Again	42
6	Talebearer	49
7	Second Meeting	59
8	Corkscrew Cottage	66
9	Confidences	74
10	Mrs. Pantanelli	83
11	The Small Boy	92
12	Nothing but Untruth	100
13	Dr. Cellini	109
14	The Essence of the Problem	119
15	The Collapse	128
16	The Woman Who Disappeared	138
17	"I Am Myself"	146
18	"Anything You Say May Be Used . . ."	154
19	The Need of Justin Gray	163
20	The Witnesses	172
21	The Wisdom of Dr. Cellini	181

Chapter 1

"THE TROUBLE WITH YOU . . ."

"THE TROUBLE WITH YOU is that you're too good to be true," Maurice Mendelson said. There was venom in his voice, rage in his eyes. "You and your bloody conscience will put us all in jail."

"Not if you drop the idea," Justin Gray said quietly.

"It's too late for that now, and you know it."

"You mean you've got yourselves into debt because you took it for granted you could swindle a client without any risk to yourselves," Justin said. "Well, you can't." After a long pause, while the three other people in the long, pleasant room stared inimically at him, he went on, "You can't even do it *with* risk."

"What the hell do you mean?" Maurice demanded fiercely.

Justin did not answer, but moved from the desk toward the window. He was aware of the appeal in Alan's eyes, the lack of expression in Hugo's sallow, aquiline face. He felt numbed because of what they had been plotting, and even the view from the window failed to soothe him. It was quite beautiful, and so unexpected. Here, on the outskirts of one of London's busiest suburbs, on the very fringe of a by-pass road often choked with traffic, was this small oasis of smooth lawns and well-tended flower beds. A patch of red roses was so near the window that it seemed almost as if he could stretch out his hand and pluck one.

Justin felt a tightness at his forehead and the back of his

head, and a numbness in his body, which held more than a threat of pain. He had felt like this often lately—too often; it was as if he were losing the control and ascendancy necessary to combat the ceaseless attempts the others made to break down his resistance.

The window was open; the breeze brought in the scent of flowers, faintly mingling with the stench of exhaust fumes. A big truck came along one of the feed roads of the roundabout, moving so fast that it seemed to be heading straight for this building. It slowed down and turned the circle, then went off along the by-pass, strangely quiet. Some acoustical trick deadened noise from the roads; and alleys between the shops—of which this was one—trapped most of the fumes. Over to the left one could see the mellowed red brick of a house, once a stately home, now a museum with relics from the Roman camp built on this very mound two thousand years ago.

The others were talking in undertones; now and again Maurice's voice rose in anger. Of the three brothers, Maurice was the prime mover in this plot, the man with the brains; Alan, younger by five years and uncannily like him, with his domed forehead and receding hair and heavy brown eyebrows, would do whatever Maurice wanted. Hugo would vacillate; he looked so incisive, so handsome, but he was almost incapable of making a decision for himself. There was only one place where he could assert himself, and that was on the stage.

He was a very capable actor, had once been a part-time professional and was now the most popular leading man in the local amateur theatrical company. Sometimes he could carry his acting over to the board room, but he cracked under the pressures of his partners' ceaseless arguments.

There was movement behind Justin.

"Justin." It was Alan, with his pleasing, pleading voice. "Won't you at least think about it?"

Justin turned, almost sadly. Alan was near him. The other

two were on either side of the board-room table, which served as a desk when it was not being used for a meeting, as it was now. Maurice was on the right, and it was easy to imagine that hatred glowed in his eyes. Hugo, opposite him, was clenching and unclenching his hands.

"No," Justin said, quite clearly, "I won't think about it at all. I simply won't do it or allow it to be done."

"But surely it won't do any harm," protested Alan. "She's so *old*. It will never be of any use to her. *She* isn't interested in making money."

It was a foolish remark, the kind that Alan uttered so often—but there was some truth in it. Mrs. Louise Pantanelli was, undoubtedly, very nearly *non compos mentis*. They all knew it. She had periods of sanity, but for the most part lived in a pleasant kind of stupor, enjoying food, watching the flicker of television without understanding, giggling when the audience laughed, otherwise watching with fatuous content.

It was bitterly ironic that she should be worth a quarter of a million pounds.

It was equally ironic that she should own some old houses on the outskirts of the suburb that, by reason of the new ring road and two light-industry factories nearly as new, had become extremely valuable. There was to be a big development, a shopping center of distinction, and Mrs. Pantanelli's houses stood in the middle of the site. Justin and Maurice had talked about this only a few days before: the land those old houses stood on must be worth fifty thousand pounds. Two years earlier they could have been bought for ten thousand.

They—the partners in Mendelson and Gray, Auctioneers and Estate Agents—were badly in need of capital. They needed it desperately to buy into other developments, which were pending. Hugo, whose handsomeness fooled so many people, was a close friend, in fact the lover, of the secretary to the town clerk of the Hodenham Council. She had advance information, which she had passed on to him. For forty thousand pounds the firm could buy land—today—that would be worth two hundred thousand in a year or two. *They* knew; no one else did. If they tried to borrow the money they would have to explain why they wanted it—and so give away the source of their secret information.

If they bought Mrs. Pantanelli's houses for, say, twelve thousand five hundred she would get a profit; and she trusted Justin implicitly. If he advised her to sell, she would undoubtedly do so.

The deal would be handled through a small trading company used for transactions that enabled the firm to reduce the burden of taxation.

Her lawyers might advise her against the sale, but they had little influence with her. She could still sign her name, and had never been certified as incapable. Her will had been made years before, and Justin was one of the trustees.

"It isn't as if we're not allowing her a profit," Alan said defensively.

"Not a bad profit, as things go—twenty-five percent appreciation. Why the devil don't you agree, Justin?" Hugo demanded. "There's nothing to stop you."

Justin said, "You know perfectly well why I won't agree. I won't act on information sneaked out in this way, and I won't cheat Mrs. Pantanelli."

"But there's no sense in refusing!" cried Hugo.

Maurice sat motionless, watching Justin—hating him. Maurice, who had always been dazzled by illusions of power bought with profits that the firm never earned; Maurice, his cousin, the son of one sister, Justin of the other.

Maurice and Justin had gurgled together, cut teeth together, crawled, staggered, walked, run, played, and gone to school together.

Such good *friends*, their mothers had glowed.

Almost like brothers, their fathers had boasted.

But they had never truly liked each other, never trusted each other; although for many years they had concealed this from their parents.

It seemed to Justin Gray that today's crisis was the inevitable climax of thirty-three years of uneasy, artificial "friendship."

"Justin, you must listen to reason." Alan tried again.

His was a facile nature. Everything would work out all right; once he conceived an idea, it became reality, no matter how often his hopes were dashed. There was no doubt that in his mind he had already spent his share of the greater income—on a boat, perhaps, or an Italian sports car.

"It won't do the old girl the slightest harm," he continued. "She'll only leave her fortune to some crazy charity. It's absolute madness to have scruples."

"After all," Maurice said in a tense voice, "you could always give your share to the Society for the Veneration of George Washington."

Justin was surprised into a laugh.

"I don't understand," Alan said blankly.

"George Washington was supposed always to tell the truth," Hugo told him irritably. "You won't improve the situation by attempting to emulate him, Justin."

"There's no way of improving the situation," Maurice said in a flat voice. "I have seen that holier-than-thou expression on our dear cousin's face before. Once there, it never rubs off. He's made up his mind, and no one is going to alter it for him—not even Justin himself. Isn't that right, Justin?" Now a sneer crept into Maurice's voice.

"No one is going to make me cheat Mrs. Pantanelli," Justin agreed. "No one is going to make me break the law, either."

"But this *wouldn't* be breaking the law!" Alan cried, with a fresh burst of eagerness. "That's the whole beauty of the scheme. It isn't a crime!"

"Justin needn't fear going to prison for it," Maurice said icily. "No one will ever be able to prove that we got advance information, and the price we're offering is fair enough on today's values."

"I simply can't understand you." Hugo stood up and moved a step toward Justin. "No one can possibly come to any harm—no one in his right senses could say that Mrs. Pantanelli would suffer in the slightest. Even if it *were* found out that we'd been tipped off, no one would blame us for taking advantage. This kind of thing is common practice."

"It is betraying trust," Justin retorted.

"Betraying trust be damned!" cried Alan. "No one will suffer, and by turning the scheme down each of us stands to lose a fortune!"

"Hardly that," Justin insisted. "We don't, in fact, stand to lose anything, for it isn't ours to lose." There was a moment's silence before he changed both tone and subject. "Shouldn't we go on to the next business—the recommended applications for mortgages, isn't it?"

"We can't leave things like this," Alan said with bitterness.

"We'll never have another opportunity like it," Hugo muttered.

They both stared at Justin, appealing, almost beseeching. Behind them, Maurice sat without expression.

The hum of traffic drifted in at the window; a wasp droned in and hovered, but no one noticed.

Justin moved to the table and sat down. With the four of them sitting there was not much room, for one wall was filled with tightly packed bookcases, another with wooden filing cabinets, a third had a long, benchlike shelf along one side that was also used for filing. It was a bright room, but the walls were stained from years of neglect and the surface of the mahogany table had lost most of the luster it ever had. Too little had been spent on maintaining either room or property.

"Don't misunderstand me," Justin said, trying to speak heartily, "I've nothing against making money! If you can bring forth a straightforward proposition, I'll be in favor of it every time. Have you those applications, Alan?"

"Yes, but—"

"I'm going to make one more effort," Hugo said. He spread his hands palms downward on the table and looked challengingly at Justin. "Make no mistake, our whole future, as individuals, as well as a firm, depends on this. All we need is your passive cooperation—you needn't take any of the money yourself, you needn't sign anything. Just approve—or at least don't object actively—and say nothing to anyone. That's all we ask—not your active participation, just passive cooperation." When there was no response, he went on with a flare of impatience, "Don't be such a humbug, Justin. Worse deals than this are going through every day."

When he stopped, Alan almost bleated, "It isn't as if anyone is going to *suffer*."

Justin sat very still. The wasp hovered over the back of his head and he could hear it droning, but no one else seemed to notice. Hugo, on one side, and Alan, on the other, were close to him. Maurice was at the opposite end of the table—his face set, his full lips pursed, the glow in his eyes baleful. This was a challenge from him to Justin. The conflict was between them as it had always been; neither of the others really mattered.

"Maurice," Justin said, "tell them they're wasting their time."

"Oh, God, what a bloody fool you are!" rasped Hugo.

"I still can't believe you'd turn down a chance like this," said Alan, with childish petulance.

"You don't know your fine, upright, righteous cousin and partner Justin," Maurice said thinly. "You don't understand the strict principles by which he lives. You aren't familiar with his code of behavior—never mind the rest of the world, let it starve, provided my conscience is clear. You've known him nearly as long as I have, but you haven't realized what a smug, pious hypocrite he is. You know as well as I do that he soils his hands on property deals that cause much more harm than this ever could. He'll apply for an eviction order for a widow with half a dozen children without turning a hair— because the law says he can. Somebody once told him that honesty is the best policy, so he invented his own particular, nauseating brand of it. He talks about betraying the trust of a senile old woman, but doesn't give a thought to betraying *us*, his own kith and kin!" Maurice paused as the others stared, then went on with restrained viciousness, "Do you know why he's really against this? Because it was my idea. He hates my guts, but he doesn't hate them anything like as much as I hate his!"

Justin, shocked in spite of what he had always known, thought with a painful echo, *hate*.

"Maurice, stop it," Alan muttered, almost frightened by the malevolence glowing in his brother's eyes.

"There's no need to make this a war," began Hugo.

"This is a war," said Maurice incisively. "Justin, for the last time, are you going to change your mind?"

"You know very well that I'm not," Justin said.

"Here's your last chance. Will you come in with us over this?" Maurice persisted.

"No," Justin said. He did not mean it to be, but his voice sounded cold and hard.

"If you don't," Maurice said, "I swear that I'll ruin you."

Justin didn't reply.

"Maurice—" Alan began.

"I shall break you," Maurice went on, with savagery as well as viciousness. "Make no mistake, I'll see that your name stinks in every nostril in Hodenham. And do you know how I'll do it? I'll show you up for the smooth-tongued, lying hypocrite that you are."

Now Alan was really shocked.

"Damn it, Maurice, don't talk like that!" He turned to Justin. "He doesn't mean it, he's just disappointed, like we all are." When no one spoke, and Justin and Maurice eyed each other, white-faced, Alan went on, "Why don't you change your mind, Justin? We don't want a family feud."

There had always been a family feud.

In a quiet, almost frightened voice, Hugo repeated, "Maurice doesn't mean what he said. He's just disappointed."

But Maurice meant every word that he had said.

Chapter 2

"THE TROUBLE WITH ME . . ."

"THE TROUBLE WITH ME," Justin Gray said under his breath, "is that I've no one to talk to."

That was only half true, of course; there was everyone to talk to: friends, family, business associates, fellow club members, even casual acquaintances. People responded readily to him, and for this he was grateful. What he couldn't do was talk about what he felt, what he thought, why he applied such a strict code of conduct to himself. He considered himself to be more objective than most people. He believed he *knew* himself. Occasionally, when something like this morning's vicious attack happened, he doubted his motives, even his behavior—but not often.

As for his appearance, he had summed it up fairly impartially. He was aware that his fair and prematurely graying hair made him look older than his years, that he was considered to be good-looking in a pleasant, unaggressive, English way; that there was a softness, a gentleness about his face that people trusted. Because of this he was the repository of many secrets—as he had been of Louise Pantanelli's before her decline had started. She had always been fond of him. The decline had been quite sudden with her: two years before she had been a bright, vital, highly intelligent woman. Then her brightness, intelligence, and vitality had been taken from her by a sudden stroke, which would have been less cruel had it killed her.

No one to talk to, Justin muttered again. No one to confide in was more truly what he meant. If only Moira had lived . . .

Well, she hadn't. In her ripening beauty, her gaiety, her gentleness, her joyous love for him, she had been struck down as swiftly as had Mrs. Pantanelli. One moment laughing, the next killed by the sudden impact of a car that had mounted the pavement without a second's warning.

It had been no one's fault, the coroner had said. Mechanical failure, the expert witness had testified. "Driver Exonerated," the local newspaper headline had announced.

Had the loss embittered him? For a while, perhaps. And although it was five years ago, he could relive the pain at moments of recollection such as this, could hear the voice on the telephone, Alan's voice, saying:

"Oh, God, Justin, something awful's happened. Moira's . . . Moira's *dead.*"

The vividness faded. Twice since then Justin had met a woman in whom he could begin to confide, but each time the memory of Moira had come between them. Only to Mrs. Pantanelli had he shown anything of what he felt.

Had he refused to enter into the plan to buy her property because of loyalty to her, personally? Or was it really a matter of principle? Had he not known her so well, would he have been so adamant?

Aloud, he said, "I hope so. My God, I hope so!"

But he couldn't be sure, and he needed someone with whom he could argue, attack, or defend his attitudes. Alone, he was aloof. He could understand Maurice's exasperation. There must be times when he seemed to behave as if he were a little tin god. "Holier than thou," Maurice had said, not for the first time. He had used the phrase as a sneer whenever Justin had thwarted him.

It was half-past six, and everyone else had left the building.

He was late, partly because he had nowhere else to go that night, partly because he had done so little during the morning that he was behind in his work. Yet he was as disinclined to get down to it now, as he had been all day. The scene with Maurice had been ugly; he was still sure that his cousin meant exactly what he said. It was nonsense, of course, and yet . . .

Was there any truth in the allegations?

Had he, Justin, become unbearably smug, self-righteous, even arrogant? Was he trying to live by standards that belonged to yesterday? At heart he was quite sure he was not, but—did others genuinely believe he was a hypocrite?

If only he could stop this absurd debating with himself!

He pulled some papers toward him, rough notes on houses that he and others had seen. Details had to be drawn up, and every particular had to be correct before prospective clients were handed a copy. *Every* particular. He found himself thinking back to one of his earlier differences with Alan, soon after he had come into the business. Alan, who had a gift for writing, had described near derelict properties as "attractive" and grown lyrical over less than ordinary houses and flats.

"But what harm can it do?" he had demanded. "It makes people want to see them."

"And then disappoints them."

"But *some* of them will see the possibilities!"

"Too many will think we're lying."

"But . . . but, damn it, this is *business!*"

Alan had cut his business teeth on Maurice, of course, but even Maurice had agreed that in this case it was folly to exaggerate.

"Justin tells the truth because he thinks it moral. I tell it because I think it pays," he had said, grinning at Justin. "Eschew highly colored descriptions of mediocre properties and you'll profit both on earth and in heaven. Eh, Justin?"

Now Justin bent to Alan's report. He might be careless over

measurements of a room, but he always saw the best features and presented them.

"*Corkscrew Cottage, a period gem,*" he had written. "*Circular staircase, seventeenth-century oak beams, twentieth-century plumbing. . . .*" Justin checked the room measurements, added details about rateable value, and put the sheet into a basket for typing. He had done two more, both straightforward, dull, and much more likely to sell quickly, when his telephone rang.

This would be someone who knew he was working late. The small switchboard was out of service at night, one line being put through to his office.

"Justin Gray," he said.

"*Who* is that?" a woman asked.

He did not recognize her voice, which was rather deep and very pleasant.

"This is Mendelson and Gray," he corrected.

"The house agents?"

"Yes, that's right."

"So you *do* live on the premises!"

"No," said Justin. "I happen to be working late, that is all. Can I help you?"

"Well, I *hope* you can, but . . ." she hesitated, then went on hurriedly, "do forgive me, but a friend recommended you, she said one of the partners lived over the offices, but if it's hopelessly late I won't bother you. I didn't really think anyone would be in."

Justin found himself chuckling. "Tell me what it is you need, and I'll tell you whether I can help."

"Well, I'm looking for a house or a cottage."

"Here in Hodenham?"

"Yes . . . or very near."

"There aren't many cottages," he told her at once. "There are a few flats—"

"No, I don't want a flat." She began to speak too quickly again. "I've come from Rhodesia and I want a small place that I can get ready for my husband when he joins me. I—oh, I *am* making a hotch-potch of this, aren't I?"

Justin laughed again. "I think I can see what you're driving at. Are you in Hodenham now?"

"Yes. I've been with friends, and I'm at the station. I *was* going to catch the seven-thirty, and then I thought it worth calling to see if by chance someone was still in your office."

"The seven-thirty to London?"

"Yes."

"There are trains every half hour," Justin told her. "Would you like to come and see me here? I can show you details of what we have available."

"You're *very* good."

"Business is business," Justin said lightly. "If you walk straight down Station Road and turn left at the T junction, you'll find our office on the right, close to the roundabout. Do you want to buy or rent?"

"Buy, preferably, if the price isn't too ruinous."

"I'll look up what we have before you arrive," promised Justin.

"That's very good of you," she said. "I'll come right away." She rang off.

Very good, very good, very good seemed to echo in Justin's ears. *Good—good—good. . . . Smug—smug—smug—smug.*

He seemed to see Maurice's face and hear his voice.

"Nonsense!" he said aloud. "This is becoming an obsession!"

He pushed his chair back and went across to the room where they had debated so hotly that morning, opened one of the wooden cabinets—and it jammed. He eased it out, and then caught his finger on a splinter. They needed steel cabinets, these were hopelessly antiquated. Too many families were living off the business, of course; two good partners could run the place easily.

Good—good—good—good.

He selected seven sets of sale particulars of two- and three-bedroom properties and put them aside, then looked through "Properties to Let." There were only two that might be suitable, and if the woman matched her voice, they probably wouldn't do for her at all.

He stepped to the window and looked toward the station.

A few youths were outside a motor accessory shop, and a woman and two children were peering into the window of a paperback bookshop next door. Farther along the road a woman was walking toward him.

She was probably the caller.

She walked well, and looked about her with obvious alertness, studying the signs on the shops and offices. Above Mendelson and Gray's swinging board she caught sight of him. He stayed long enough to wave, then took the files downstairs. By the time he had put them on a desk in the back office she was at the door, which had one large glass panel.

She was smiling pleasantly.

Mentally, he put one of the flats and two of the houses back in the files; they would be of no interest to her. He unlocked the door and they stood for a moment on either side of the threshold. Then Justin put out his hand.

"I'm Justin Gray."

"I'm Charlotte Warwick."

"Do come in." He stood aside for her to pass.

"I really *am* grateful."

"Don't be, until I've been useful!"

"So . . . so few people seem ready to put themselves out," she said, and then gave a little, apologetic laugh. "Or shouldn't I say that?"

"Why not, if it's true?"

"I find that the English don't relish the truth as much as they used to."

They both laughed.

"There speaks a colonial," he suggested.

Her face lit up. "You mean you actually *call* us colonials, not citizens of an emergent nation? That's so rare I can hardly believe it!"

"Have we really become as pompous as that?" Justin asked, half seriously.

Sobering, too, she said, "Some of you have, I'm afraid."

"It's puzzling," remarked Justin.

"Well, I suppose it's just grown on you."

"I mean, why you want to live here." He kept a straight face, and she searched it as if half afraid that he had taken offense. They were quiet for a moment, and then he said, "It works only if it cuts two ways."

"If what—oh! If you can be forthright with me, too?"

"That's right." It was good to see how quick her mind was.

"The awful truth . . ." she began, but hesitated.

"Go on."

"I really mustn't go too far!"

"Try me."

"All right, I will," she said, but still hesitated.

She had very clear, amber-colored eyes. Her hair, a near-auburn, was not as dark as he had thought. Her skin was clear but pale, and she wore little makeup except lipstick, which seemed to him too vivid and too thick; but, glistening, it emphasized her full lips, uptilted at the corners. Her nose was short, the nostrils slightly distended.

"What is so difficult?" he asked.

"I suppose you've been so nice I'm beginning to wonder whether I've judged you too hastily." She threw up her hands. "Oh well, it isn't a *crime* not to want to come back to England."

"Don't you want to?" he asked.

"I *hate* the thought of it!"

"Are we really as bad as that?" asked Justin again, and this time he was almost shocked. "Is that what you think of us abroad?"

She hesitated before saying, "An awful lot of us do. But that's not the only reason I don't want to live here." She looked rather bleakly out of the window. "This is only the third warm day in the month I've been here, and I've lived in a hot climate for ten years."

"Where?" he asked.

"Rhodesia."

"Salisbury? Bulawayo?"

"No, up in the hills, near Umtali."

"I know Umtali," he said.

"Why then you must know—" She broke off, as if in distress. "But here am I, gossiping, when you've stayed late to show me some houses."

"There's still over an hour of daylight," Justin pointed out. "We can have a quick look at them all. I'll get the keys while you glance at these." He went into the outer office, unlocked the case where the keys were kept, selected those he wanted, and dropped them into his pocket, then went back to the smaller office. Charlotte Warwick was reading one of the sets of particulars.

"Which one is that?" Justin asked.

"Next door to the cemetery."

"As my cousin Alan would say, a spacious view," Justin said with a smile. "It isn't too bad, really. Let's go." He stepped across and opened the door—and then stopped in his tracks.

A dead dog, bloodied and broken, lay in the porch close to the door.

Chapter 3

SENT WITH MALICE

JUSTIN FELT his body going tense, his hands clenching. Charlotte, moving toward the door, missed a step and asked in a breathless way:

"What is it? What's the matter?" She glanced down. "Oh, my God!"

She held her hands in front of her as if to push the body away or to hide it from her sight. Two or three people passed, a car roared, and a red sports car with the engine suddenly racing flashed by. Justin saw the flash of red without realizing its possible significance.

"Go inside," he said, and then his voice changed. "Or would you rather go back to London?"

"Why . . ." she began, but stopped. "What are you going to do?"

"Move this."

"Can't I help?"

He hesitated, and then said, "If you walk to the end of the passage and unlock the back door, I'll be grateful."

"Of course," she said in turn.

He left the door open and went to a cupboard where packing material was kept, took out a large piece of brown paper and carried it to the door. Three small boys, hair cut short, jerseys tight around plump bodies, were looking aghast at the dog.

"It's *dead*," one said in a whisper.

"Is it yours?" Justin asked heavily.

"No—we just seed it," one boy answered.

"Did you see how it got here?" asked Justin.

"It must have been run over," hazarded the middle boy.

"Did it just crawl here and *die?*" asked the first.

Justin said, "Did you *see* anything?"

"No, sir. What are you going to do with it?" the boy asked.

"Put it in my garden."

"Are you going to leave it there?"

"Yes," Justin said gently.

It had been put here, of course, quite deliberately. As he covered the body with the brown paper, tucking it in as well as he could, then took off his jacket and draped it over a chair, thoughts flashed through his mind of the day, three or four years ago, when he had run over a dog and killed it. It had taken him days to recover from the shock, and everything that had happened now came back vividly.

Maurice had been with him.

Maurice had just passed, in his red TR-3.

Justin bent down and worked the paper farther under the body. He noticed there was no collar; this looked like a stray. Two women and an old man joined the trio of boys watching him. He carried the body through the outer office, along the passage, and into the garden. Charlotte was standing beneath an apple tree, near a burned patch where an incinerator stood, with pale blue smoke curling up from it.

"Where are you going to put it?" she asked.

"Over by the fence, on the patch of concrete," he said.

"Oughtn't you to bury it?"

"Not yet."

"I don't mind waiting."

"The owner might want to look after it," Justin pointed out.

"Oh yes," she said. "I hadn't thought of that."

She watched him soberly as he lowered his burden, completely covered, then placed bricks on the corners of the paper, holding it down. When he straightened up, Charlotte's eyes were turned toward him, puzzled, her expression speculative and thoughtful.

"If you'd rather not go out—"

"I'll wash and be ready in five minutes," Justin promised.

"May I wait out here?"

"Of course."

There were other back gardens, outhouses, trees, washing on several lines, the humming of wasps and buzzing of flies; all, but for the pitiful parcel, pleasant enough. He washed at a sink overlooking the garden, saw Charlotte looking about her, glancing only now and then at the dog.

He went out, calling her.

The three small boys and the old man were all there, still standing by the door when they left, all talking animatedly. Justin locked the door as a boy called:

"Did you bury it?"

"Not yet," Justin said.

He put a hand at Charlotte's elbow, guiding her along the narrow street. His pale gray Morris 1800 was the third car along. He unlocked the door and closed it after she had got in, took the wheel, and started off smoothly.

"I'm really sorry about that," he said.

"You don't have to be. It wasn't even remotely your fault."

He didn't respond.

"Do you know who it was?" she asked.

"I can guess," he said heavily. Maurice, of course, beginning to get his revenge. If he informed the police they would have to be told of his suspicions . . .

"What a beastly thing to do!" the woman exclaimed.

"There's a lot of beastliness in some people," he remarked bitterly.

"Has it happened before?" she asked with sudden suspicion.

"No, nothing like it."

"Do you—" She broke off, and rested a hand lightly on his arm. "I'm sorry, it's no business of mine.

"It should never have happened," he said gruffly. "Let's stop talking about it, shall we?"

"We *were* talking about something else. I've forgotten what it was."

"About people I must know in or near Umtali," he reminded her.

"Oh yes! Goodness, what a memory you have!"

"For some things," he answered.

"What were you doing in Umtali?"

"Just looking around," Justin told her.

He could have added that when he had gone there three years ago, considering the possibility of buying some land and settling there, he had done so out of distress at the conditions in England. But he had not been able to make the wrench, his roots being more deeply planted than he had thought. He turned now into a road with a green and pleasant cemetery along one side and slowed down.

"It *isn't* as depressing as it sounds," she said.

"No, it's very lovely in its way."

Over there, within sight, was Moira's grave. Usually he could pass this spot without emotional distress, just a kind of sadness, but today it hurt.

He pulled up outside a small house standing in a quarter of an acre of garden, the windows blank-looking and curtainless. A "For Sale" notice stood on a post by the front gate.

"Mr. Gray?"

"Yes?"

"Will you forgive me if we don't go in? I couldn't live here."

"Then it would be a waste of time going in," Justin said. "It's the best of the houses, though."

"It looks nice, but . . ."

He took her to the other houses, their footsteps echoing on bare, dusty boards. In each of them there was a musty air, a forlorn emptiness; in one, a few toys in a corner spoke of life and eagerness that had once been there.

They finished when dusk was falling.

"I'm awfully sorry, but they simply won't do," Charlotte said.

"And I'm sorry because there's nothing else I can show you," said Justin. "There isn't a great deal of development in the town except in one area, and there the prices are sky-high—you did say you wanted it for only a few years, didn't you?"

Charlotte answered, "Did I?"

"Perhaps I misunderstood you."

"Much more likely, I was vague. To be more precise, I have six months to get a house, or home, for my husband, who will by then have finished a job and be ready to take up a three-year appointment in England. So I need it for at least three and a half years."

"Must it be at Hodenham, or very close?"

"It has to be on this side of London—my husband's appointment is at Roehampton Hospital."

"The rehabilitation place?" Justin asked with interest.

"Yes."

"It's wonderful work," he said warmly.

"It is indeed," said Charlotte Warwick. There was something in her tone that Justin didn't understand. "My husband is a wonderful man." After a pause, she went on, "And I have friends here, or I thought I had. Am I being painfully obscure?"

"Obscure, yes," said Justin, "but there's no reason why you

shouldn't be. Forgive me, but when I'm interested I'm inclined to probe. A bad habit."

"Oh, don't worry about that. A school friend of mine lives near here, out at Ringborn." Ringborn was a newly developed area, within the Hodenham boundaries. "She came out to stay with me with her first husband, but she's divorced and married again and—it isn't the same. As a matter of fact I telephoned you only because I didn't want to waste the rest of the day." She laughed, rather wryly. "If you had the right house I *would* come here. Having a settled home would be a kind of life line."

"Not your husband?" Justin hardly knew what prompted him to ask that.

After a pause, she said, "He's always very busy."

The implication was that he neglected her. It flashed through Justin's mind that it must surely be an insensitive man who would neglect a woman of such quality and attractiveness, but as he turned into the traffic circle a red sports car cut across him and he had to brake swiftly. *Maurice,* he thought—and then saw a fair-haired youth at the wheel, a blonde's head on his shoulder.

He pulled up outside the offices.

"We can do two things," he said. "I can leave the keys here, I need only drop them through the letter box, and take you to the station. You'll catch the eight-thirty train then. Or we could have dinner first, and I could drive you to town later."

She was looking at him, and her eyes lit up. "That sounds lovely!"

"Then I'll drop the keys in," he declared. When he took the wheel again, he went on, "There's a pleasant little pub about five miles out where the food is plain but good, and the people might help to restore your faith in the English!"

Very quietly she said, "A lot of my faith in the English has already been restored." As he started off, she asked, "But aren't I taking up too much of your time?"

"You're a boon," he said, "especially to a bachelor who lives on eggs cooked every known and unknown way, cheese, fruit, and coffee. I seldom go out to a meal."

"Oh, but you should!"

"I'm going to, tonight," he reminded her.

They drove along narrow roads in an area that was almost rural, past houses of good quality standing back from the road, then into a village almost unspoiled, with a thatched-roofed inn on one side and a few small shops opposite. At the front of the inn was a mass of varicolored flowers planted in an old horse trough. A huge pale blue hydrangea stood at the main door. Inside, it was much more spacious than it appeared from the road. A bar ran along one wall, the bottles behind it glowing with the colors of wines and brandies, whiskeys and liqueurs. The tables were opposite the bar, and an elderly man came up, dressed in a starched white dinner jacket.

"For two, Mr. Gray?"

"Please, George."

"Can you wait about fifteen minutes, until the dining room is open, sir?"

"Yes, of course."

"If you'd like to study the menu while you are waiting . . ."

They ordered iced melon and Aylesbury duckling in orange sauce, had a drink, ate and talked idly, and were still there when the pub had to close. The night was clear beneath bright stars, the scent of tobacco plants and night-scented stock heavy on the warm air.

Justin had forgotten the dog. He had forgotten what it was like to relax in such unthinking peace and contentment.

He was sorry to have to pull up outside a building emblazoned with the words "Outram Hotel" in Kensington. He got out and opened the door for Charlotte and strolled with her to the entrance. A youthful-looking night porter, Indian or Pakistani, opened the doors.

"Justin," Charlotte said, turning to him on the porch, "it's been absolutely lovely. Thank you *so* much."

"It's been enchanting," Justin told her. "Come and look for more houses in Hodenham, won't you?"

"The moment you tell me there's something available," she promised. "Good night."

His "good night" followed her toward the lift.

He turned away, his mood changing, feeling lost and lonely as he got back to the car. By the time he reached Hodenham it was nearly one o'clock; he was tired, and he could not keep the thought of the quarrel with Maurice, or the pitiful body of the dead dog, out of his mind. There was little doubt that Maurice had arranged for someone to put the dog there. . . . It was sickening.

He garaged the car at the side of the big house where he had a flat, one with its own door, every facility he could want, and a view over the distant countryside that, in Alan's parlance, would put thousands of pounds onto its value. He walked to the door, keys jingling in his hand, reminded of Charlotte by the perfume of night-scented stock that grew in a border about the lawn.

As he drew close to the door he kicked against something heavy, and it threw him forward. He banged his head against the door, and the pain made it difficult for him to keep his balance. Trying to do so, he trod on whatever was in front of the door.

It was soft and yielding.

He thought, It *can't* be—he wouldn't do it *twice.*

But he knew that he was treading on the body of yet another dead dog, a dog that had been placed there to make him fall, and to chill him with horror.

It was a white dog, smaller than the first, showing hardly any signs of injury.

He carried it to the hedge, then went slowly, almost fearfully, to his flat.

Chapter 4

DENIAL

HE LAY AWAKE for a long time, but at last dropped into a heavy sleep. Yet he was awake again before half-past seven, in time to switch his alarm off before the bell rang. He lay half dozing for a while, slowly recollecting what had happened—but the pleasure of reliving his evening with Charlotte Warwick was almost entirely spoiled by the memory of the two dogs, and the motive that lay behind their deaths. He had the kettle on and was brushing his teeth when it flashed into his mind that Maurice, in pursuit of his plan, might deliberately have killed the dogs.

Could he really be as cold-blooded as that?

Justin could recall Maurice tormenting flies, wasps, bees, birds; could remember him watching trapped moths and butterflies with enjoyment, never thinking of releasing them. In those early days of boyhood such things had happened often. Justin could remember Maurice jeering, scoffing, when he had protested.

"They can't *feel*, not like we can."

They could, and he had known it.

Justin had sensed the cruelty, tried to stop it, and finally accepted it as part of Maurice's makeup. Some people were like that, others were different, they could not hurt a fly. He had not thought of it in terms of being good or bad until a long time afterward, and by that time Maurice seemed to have grown out of his acts of cruelty.

But now Maurice would torment girls—young, pretty girls, who loved or thought they loved him. He had a kind of mesmeric effect on them. When they were with him he could do what he liked with them—and afterward taunt them with their own folly.

"My God, a girl of your age ought to be able to look after herself."

"But you said you loved me . . . you said—"

"Well, you didn't believe *that*, did you?" Maurice would say, laughing harshly. "Don't be such a little fool." Now and again when a girl had been to his office, anguished and afraid, Justin had heard such talk.

His morning tea was tasteless.

Before shaving, while the bath was running, he looked out of the window. The pale hindquarters of the dog showed beneath the shiny green of the hedge; this garden was communal, he couldn't leave the body there. He made himself eat toast and marmalade, then went downstairs. There was no mail for him; there seldom was these days. He took a cardboard carton from a shed, put the corpse into it, and placed it in the trunk of his car, noticing that there was no collar on this one either. No one was about, although the day was already warm and fine. He drove to the office and carried the carton along an alley to the back garden. There was a steady stream of people heading for work; he could hear their footsteps. Almost without conscious thought he took a spade and began to dig. The ground was hard from its rare need of rain, and before he had finished a shallow hole he was sweating freely.

He placed both bodies in it and covered them first with sprays of leaves, then with loose earth. He should really report this second macabre happening to the police, but it would only involve Maurice, and he hated the thought of that. The owners of the dogs would advertise, if they thought enough of their pets, and he would watch the local newspaper. If both were strays . . .

He had made the hole shallow; they could be uncovered

without difficulty. When at last he had finished he felt greater nausea than ever and went behind the apple tree and was violently sick.

He felt weak and spiritless when at last he went into the office.

The keys, with some mail, were on the mat. He put the keys back into position mechanically, then put the particulars on a girl's desk for filing. He went upstairs, his footsteps dragging. It was only ten to nine, but some of the staff should be here by now—the senior clerk, a woman named Bertha Briggs, would be first to open the front door. Two other girls and a youth made up the rest of the staff.

Too many fed off this business, Justin reminded himself; two of the partners ought to go. Then there would be a fair income for everybody.

He should go. He knew it. He faced the fact that there was little or no chance of getting along with the others now. He had not faced up to this before, but there was no longer any way of avoiding it. It was not simply that they had had a difference of opinion; it had been a deep and bitter conflict of principles. Even without Maurice's vendetta, the chance of a smooth-running partnership was negligible. It wasn't, formally, a partnership. They simply worked together, having inherited a quarter interest each. Even if they drew up a deed of partnership it would not help unless they all got on well together.

He heard the shop doorbell go and Bertha Briggs bustle in. He got up and called:

"I'm in my office, Bertha."

"I thought it was you, Mr. Gray. I'll bring your mail up as soon as I can."

"Let me know when Mr. Maurice comes in, will you?"

"Yes, sir, I will."

He looked through the notes, from which he had drawn up

the particulars of yesterday's properties, thinking suddenly that Charlotte Warwick might be interested in Corkscrew Cottage—he should have thought of it last night.

The front doorbell rang several times again.

Alan came in and leaped up the stairs, whistling. Usually he put his head around the door, but this morning he simply paused for a moment, and then passed by. A few moments later, at half-past nine, Hugo came in, went past Justin's to Alan's office, and began to talk about a rehearsal for A *Taste of Honey*. Soon he began to talk about a threatened airlines' strike.

"If the louts *do* strike, that will be the end of *my* summer holiday," he complained.

"Shouldn't go so far in your woman-hunting," Alan retorted. He was the only one of the partners who was married. "Try Bournemouth or Brighton for a change. British belles are every bit as beautiful."

"It's all very well for you," said Hugo. "I'm pretty fed up about it, I can tell you. If it isn't one thing it's another." He lowered his voice. "Seen Justin?"

"No."

"Maurice isn't in, I see."

Maurice had a small ground-floor office at one side, and could be seen through the glass panel of its door. There was another door to this office from the street, and Maurice often used that.

"He will be," Alan said disinterestedly.

"Yes. He pitched it pretty strong yesterday."

"Justin asked for it."

"Shut up, you ass! He might hear you."

"I don't give a damn whether he hears me or not," Alan growled. "To put that senile old woman before us—my God, he must be mad."

"Or else he hates our guts."

"Or *Maurice's* guts."

"That's what Maurice thinks—that it's personal," said Hugo. "You don't think Maurice was serious when he said he'd ruin Justin, do you?"

"I think he was deadly serious, and if he wants help from me, he'll get it," replied Alan sourly. "I know the first thing I would do."

"What would you do?"

"Get rid of Justin."

"For Pete's sake—he might *hear* you."

"I don't give a damn whether he hears me or not," repeated Alan. "He proved yesterday that he hasn't got the firm's interests at heart. If I had my way, he'd be out on his neck *now*."

"We can't very well get rid of him," protested Hugo, but his voice was weak; obviously he was becoming impressed by the idea.

"We can make life so difficult for him he'll be glad to resign," said Alan.

"I wish you wouldn't talk so loudly," Hugo protested.

The telephone on Justin's desk rang. He let it ring for a few moments, sickened by what he had overheard. Slowly he picked up the receiver. Bertha Briggs' voice came primly over the wire.

"I haven't got all the mail opened, but Mr. Maurice is in, sir."

"Thanks, Bertha," Justin said.

He stood up stiffly and moved to the door.

"Well, time for the treadmill," Hugo boomed, his back turned toward Justin as his door opened wider.

To reach the top of the stairs Justin had to pass Alan's office. Glancing in, he saw Alan drop his eyes studiously to his desk. Downstairs a typewriter began to chatter: that would be

Bertha; the other girls could do little more than hunt and peck for the keys. Though it was now well after ten o'clock, only Bertha would have done any serious work.

He went downstairs.

Maurice, who dealt with the loans and Building Society side of the business, had selected his office because of the second doorway. Through this a steady stream of borrowers came each day to make their payments on houses bought against mortgages usually too heavy for the borrowers to bear. He had one girl clerk during the week who worked at the counter, and he had a small box of an office for himself.

Justin went in.

Maurice was sitting at his desk, lighting a cigarette. He took longer than he needed, leisurely sliding his lighter into a side pocket. He looked up.

"Are you still with us?"

"Yes," Justin said, "and likely to be for a long time."

"I quite expected you to desert the ship you're so intent on sinking," Maurice sneered. "Or are you waiting to watch us drown?"

Justin said, "Your own taste in that line so far exceeds my own, it would be folly to compete."

Maurice looked at him from under his lashes. His eyes were half hidden, and what Justin could see of his face was very pale.

He said, "I don't think I like that remark."

"Nor do I like having the corpses of dogs flung onto my doorstep."

Maurice started. "*What* did you say?"

"You heard me."

"The corpses of *what* dogs?"

"Those you put on the porch here and at my flat door last night."

Slowly, Maurice leaned back, took the cigarette from his lips, and said, "Don't be a bloody fool."

"Don't lie to me, Maurice."

"*I* don't know anything about any dead dogs."

"You either put them there or you paid someone to do it."

Maurice put the cigarette back to his lips and shook his head with great deliberation. He did not shift his gaze from Justin, but that meant nothing. As a boy he could lie with the greatest aplomb, utterly convincing anyone who did not know him well.

"Not I," he stated.

"I don't believe you," retorted Justin.

"I don't care what you believe," Maurice said. "I was out with a girl last night, and far too busy to worry about dead dogs, or cats or ducks for that matter. You didn't seem to be doing so badly yourself. I saw you coming out of the Rose and Crown." He paused, and then added, "Who was she, by the way? Do I smell romance?"

"You might smell a customer," Justin said. "Maurice, don't ever play that kind of trick on me again."

"*I* haven't played any trick," Maurice said lightly. "If you'd seen my strawberry blonde last night, you would know why. Have you changed your mind about Mrs. P.'s property?"

"No."

"You'd better," said Maurice, his voice deepening. "You'd certainly better."

"You know perfectly well that I won't make any concessions to dishonest or corrupt practice."

"If you haven't changed your mind and come in with us before the day's out," Maurice said, "I'll run you out of this town. I won't do it by leaving dead dogs on your doorstep, either. Now if you haven't any business to discuss, I've work to do."

"Yes," Justin said. "I've business to discuss."

"What?"

"You are taking too much money out of the company for the effort you put into it," Justin said flatly. "You were gone by four o'clock yesterday. You weren't in until ten o'clock this morning. If you would put a fair day's work into the job there wouldn't be any crisis—even *you* wouldn't need to cheat an old woman." Maurice looked so startled that he went on, "Hugo is as bad. The only one of you who justifies his money is Alan, and he can't always do his own job properly because he's covering up for you or Hugo. It's time it stopped."

Maurice gasped, "Why, you've got a nerve!"

"What I've got is a quarter share in a business that ought to be doing well but is doing badly because two of my partners are parasites," Justin accused.

He watched Maurice glowering, now thoroughly incensed, then turned on his heel and went out. Just outside the door was plump Bertha Briggs, who looked at him from behind the pebble lenses of her glasses, as if with approval. Could she have overheard?

Whether she had or not, one thing was certain. He and Maurice were at war, and one or the other would have to lose. He felt curiously elated, almost glad that the latent antagonism between them had been brought to the surface. And now the issue had been forced, the tension was likely to grow until the struggle was over. The mood continued; he sensed that he had been aware that the situation would have to come to a head eventually, that the clash over Mrs. Pantanelli's property was the excuse, not the reason, for Maurice's attitude.

Bertha brought up his letters; he dealt with most of the properties for sale, negotiated with lawyers, and arranged all property and furniture for auction. He knew that he found more work to do, proportionately, than any of the partners, but even so, there was time on his hands. Because of that he was able to take on a great deal of social work, serve on a dozen committees, help with special charity appeals.

One letter was from the mayor's office.

Dear Mr. Gray,

For my special mayoral effort this year, I have decided to make a Community Appeal for Cancer Research, and think a target of £5,000 might be reasonable. I hope very much you will serve on the Appeals Committee, and if you are able to, hope you can come here on Friday, 23 June, at 5:30 P.M. to discuss the campaign with me and other helpers.

Yours sincerely,
Jacob R. Frimly,
Mayor.

Almost without thinking, Justin thumbed through his diary; it did not occur to him to refuse or even hesitate; it was simply a matter of whether he had any other appointment at that time. He read:

Library Committee, Town Hall, 3 P.M.
Road Accident Committee, Town Hall, 4:15 P.M.
Cricket Club Summer Ball, 8:00 P.M.

He penciled in, Mayor's Cancer Committee, 5:30 P.M., closed his diary, and was about to draft a note of acceptance for one of the girls to type when his telephone bell rang.

"Hello," he said.

"There's a Mrs. Warwick on the line, sir. Will you speak to her?" a girl asked.

Justin hesitated, and then said evenly, "Yes, put her through." He was astonished at the way his heart thudded, and the excitement that he felt.

Chapter 5

CHARLOTTE AGAIN

"Is this Justin Gray?"

"Charlotte, how nice to hear from you!"

Charlotte's laugh carried relief. It was obvious that she had been a little on edge when she had first called.

"I wanted so much to thank you for last night," she said.

"There's nothing at all to thank me for. I enjoyed every minute."

Almost as soon as he said that he had a mental image of the dog on the porch, and shied away from it.

She said quickly, "*Every* minute?"

"Every minute that mattered," he answered more quietly.

"Justin, that was such a beastly thing to happen."

"Yes . . . but please don't worry about it."

"It's difficult not to," she said. "I couldn't bring myself to say much last night, but I saw how shocked you were. Do you . . . ?" she hesitated.

"You really needn't worry about it," he insisted.

"Do you know who was responsible?"

"Someone with a macabre sense of humor, evidently," he answered.

"Humor," she echoed, and this time her laugh had an edge to it. "That kind of thing should never happen to anyone . . . much less to you."

"Oh, come!" he protested. "You hardly know me."

"I know you well enough to be sure of that," she said, and then her tone changed and she began to speak much more quickly and brightly. "But I didn't mean to talk about *that*. I wanted to say 'thank you' for a lovely evening, and for all the trouble you took."

"I'd be happy to take that kind of trouble for that kind of evening any time," he said. He knew that he sounded glib, yet he had seldom meant anything more seriously.

"Whenever you find a house that might do for me—"

"Good Lord!" interjected Justin. "I'd forgotten again. There *is* such a house; I didn't think of it last night. You might find it's exactly what you want. Genuine period, tiny, with a small garden and almost a view. *Not* of the cemetery, either!"

Charlotte said, "That sounds too good to be true."

The phrase struck sharply at him, with a mocking echo. "Too good to be true," Maurice had sneered. "You're too good to be true."

After a slight pause, he said evenly, "You might even like the name—Corkscrew Cottage."

"I do like the name," she declared at once.

"When can you come and see it?"

"When can you show it to me?"

"Let me check my diary," he said. "Hold on." Muttering to himself, he went on, "Museum Committee 5 P.M., Theatre Committee 7:15. I can cut that." Because it was summer there were fewer evening meetings than usual. Aloud, he suggested, "Tonight?"

"If you really have to cut a meeting . . ." she began hesitantly.

"I really don't have to go," he assured her. "Can you be here at six o'clock?"

"Yes, of course. Shall I come to the office?"

"Will you?"

"Of course," she said again. "Justin, thank you so much. And forgive me for the horrid things I said last night."

"You were only being colonial," he said with assumed sobriety.

They were both laughing as they rang off.

He sat back, looking at the diary on his desk, and slowly his smile changed to a frown. He pulled it to him and skimmed the entries in the earlier part of the year. There were days when he was at committee meetings from lunchtime onward, times when he had to slip back to the office, sign the letters, and rush off again. What right had he to tell Maurice and the others they were not pulling their weight in the business? They chose to play golf, or cricket, or tennis; to fish; to take long weekends, Maurice and Hugo with girl friends who seemed never to be the same two weeks running. What they did was their affair. A man's morality was his own, and he, Justin, did not feel strongly critical about the peccadillos of his partners.

The strength of his feeling on personal honesty and integrity was another matter.

Hypocrite, Maurice had called him; humbug. Was that so unjustified? If he added up the actual hours he spent on business affairs, would the total be much greater than that of the others? True, he had been coming back into the office during the evenings in the summer, but this was at least as much because he was at loose ends as because he was concerned for the firm.

He turned a page.

"Road Safety Conference, Eastbourne," he read. "Wednesday / Saturday, April 23–26."

Who was he to talk about long weekends?

The reflections did only a little to spoil his pleasure at Charlotte Warwick's call. By the time his morning coffee was brought to him, he was wondering where to take Charlotte to dinner.

He could suggest his flat, for he could broil a steak as well or better, than most. He must remember to slip back and take a couple of steaks out of the freezer. He was interrupted by a call from a London firm of agents about an auction they were holding jointly in a few weeks time. Clients drifted in. He went out with two of them; one was more than slightly interested in the house overlooking the cemetery, and it was midday before he got back to the flat and put the steaks out. He checked the vegetables, put a bottle of Pouilly-Fuissé in the refrigerator, stood a half bottle of Nuits St. George on the sideboard, then returned to the office.

There, on his desk, was a dead sparrow.

The bird's body was warm. There was no outward sign of injury. It looked as if it had flown at full speed against a window, and broken its neck. He slid a piece of stiff paper under, folded this, and carried it from his office. Alan and Hugo were out at lunch, but he could hear voices at Maurice's door. Bertha, who missed little despite her short-sightedness, asked:

"Can I help you, Mr. Justin?"

"Who's with Mr. Maurice, do you know?"

"It's Mr. Goldworth, of Eagle Building Society. They're going out to lunch at one o'clock."

"Then I won't disturb them. Bertha, who's been upstairs while I've been out?"

Bertha frowned and then asked very quietly, "Why, sir?"

"I would like to know."

She took off her glasses, showing eyes buried deep in a puffy face. Once she had been pretty; now her only indulgence was food and television in the evenings. She was a prodigious worker, and if anything happened to her it would spell disaster for Mendelson and Gray.

She said quietly, "All the other partners have been upstairs. There has been a conference of some kind."

"And the staff?"

"Lucy went up to Mr. Alan and I've been up several times," said Bertha. "Why, Mr. Justin? What's happened?" She looked anxious, even distressed. "Nothing's missing, is it?"

"No," Justin said. "Have any strangers been in the front office?"

"Well, yes, the usual half dozen or so who are looking for somewhere to live," answered Bertha. "Mr. Justin, I don't like to say it again, but unless we keep that back door locked there's absolutely *no* way of being sure the place is secure. You really ought to have a new lock put on, change the keys, and *keep* it locked."

"You're probably right," Justin temporized.

"I *know* I'm right," asserted Bertha stubbornly. "After all, *I'm* responsible if anything goes wrong, and I've only got one pair of eyes."

"I'll talk to the partners about it," Justin promised.

"That's what you *always* say, sir, but nothing ever gets done. I sometimes wish"—Bertha's eyes were sparkling, and she was speaking with unusual feeling, as if she had been upset by someone or something else and was taking it out on him—"I sometimes wish the partners would show a greater sense of responsibility, sir. I really do."

For Bertha, that was almost a revolutionary remark. Justin wondered what had upset her, whether Maurice had been complaining about something not done; he could anger a saint when he was in the mood.

Making himself smile, he said jestingly, "We're a poor lot, Bertha, aren't we?"

"That is as may be," Bertha said shortly. "But I don't know what would happen to this place without me—and goodness knows I don't get much thanks for it."

She turned and went back into the front office.

Justin, shaken by the outburst, went out of the back door and placed the dead sparrow in the hedge not far from the spot where he had buried the dogs. As he turned around, he had a swift mental picture of Charlotte standing beneath the apple tree, bright, eager, alert—very different from anyone in the office, incredibly different from Bertha, very different, too, from slim-built, childlike Moira.

The back door ought to be kept locked, but it was convenient to keep it unlocked. It was quite true that anyone could walk along the alley, come into the back door, run upstairs, and be down again without anyone having seen them. Presumably someone had done that with the sparrow. Either that, or one of the cousins . . .

It was hard to believe this of anyone except Maurice—and even he would hardly take the risk of being caught in the act. He *must* have employed someone to take care of the two dogs, and possibly the same person had brought the sparrow.

How could he, Justin, find out?

On the spur of the moment he hurried up to his room and telephoned the local police headquarters. Hodenham was a subdivision of the Metropolitan Police, with an inspector—Malleson—in charge, two criminal investigation sergeants, two detective officers, and several uniformed men. Justin knew Malleson quite well; they played tennis and occasionally billiards, served on several committees together, and each belonged to the Hodenham Rotary Club.

"Is Inspector Malleson there, please?"

"Yes. Who wants him?"

"Justin Gray."

"Just a moment, Mr. Gray."

There was a long pause, almost long enough to make Justin restive, before Malleson came on the line, brisk-voiced, with a faint north-country accent.

"Hello, Justin. What can I do for you?"

"Have lunch with me, or spare me twenty minutes immediately afterward," Justin said.

"Provided it doesn't take too long, let's have lunch," said Malleson. "I want to talk to you, anyhow—we've had an anonymous report that you've been burying bodies in your garden!"

Chapter 6

TALEBEARER

Eric Malleson was short for a policeman, barely five feet eight, but solid and broad-shouldered. He had a broad face, a slightly sallow complexion, black hair cut short, and a darkly shadowed chin. His eyes were small and deep-set; a lot of people who met him for the first time distrusted him, but he had been in charge of the subdivisional station for eight years and established himself as a likable, active, forthright man.

Yet by the very nature of his job there were some reservations about him, and Justin was acutely aware of that as he watched him walk across the restaurant attached to the Sports Club. This was at the far side of the park from Mendelson and Gray's offices—ten minutes walk along well-tended paths, flower beds, and lawns.

The men shook hands and sat down. They had been allotted a table in a corner, away from anyone else, and an open window overlooked the cricket ground and four grass tennis courts, each occupied by players.

Anticipating their order, a waitress brought two half-pint tankards of light ale.

"Cheers," Malleson said, and drank deeply.

"Cheers. What's all this about an anonymous report?"

"Shall we order first and talk while we're eating?" suggested Malleson. "It's hot for steak pudding, but if it's on, that's for me."

"I'll go along with it, too," said Justin. The waitress came up. "Steak pudding for us both, Maude."

"Have to be pie," said Maude lugubriously.

"That'll do."

"Have to." Malleson leaned back in his chair.

"Anything to start with?"

"No thanks, love," Malleson said. He waited until she was out of earshot, then turned to Justin. "What do you want to talk about, Justin?"

Justin hesitated, and then said, "Dead bodies."

"So it was true?"

"The report—yes. I buried two dogs this morning."

"Wasn't that overdoing it a bit?" asked Malleson.

"I don't quite follow."

"They weren't yours, were they?"

"No."

Malleson drank again, then lowered his tankard and looked at Justin. He didn't smile. His stare was not one of accusation, but there was something slightly censorious in his manner.

"You don't make a habit of killing and burying stray dogs, do you?"

Justin didn't respond at once, taken aback by the phrase "killing and burying." The word "killing" had an ugly ring, and there was something inimical in the way Malleson used it.

He put his tankard down as deliberately as had Malleson.

"I didn't kill the dogs. Did your anonymous informant accuse me of killing them?"

"Yes," Malleson answered bluntly.

"Have you any idea who called you?"

"None at all. If you didn't kill them, Justin, why bury them?"

"That is why I wanted to see you," Justin said. He felt slightly at a loss. This was an Eric Malleson he had observed in action with others, but never known himself. "I'm worried and puzzled, and I thought you might help—unofficially, of course."

"If it's a police matter, you know very well I can't act unofficially," Malleson pointed out.

"You could advise unofficially, surely?"

"Supposing you tell me what it's all about, and then I can answer," said Malleson.

Justin hesitated.

What he really wanted was to spy on his partners—his cousins. There was no certainty, as yet, that it was a police matter, but Eric might now feel as if he had to treat it as such. Justin felt chilled by the inspector's manner, and wished very much that he hadn't made the approach. As if divining his thoughts, the policeman relaxed a little.

"Once I had the message, I would in any case have come to see you," he said. "Presumably you'd have told me the whole story if I'd made the first approach."

"I suppose so," Justin said slowly. "I don't know. The fact is . . ." He saw the waitress bearing down on them and waited until she had gone. The aroma that rose from the rich brown meat and gravy was tempting enough to drive recollection of the heat away. "The fact is," he repeated, "I don't want to make this an official complaint. I simply want some advice, and if necessary, help." He held Malleson's gaze for a few seconds, then looked down at his plate.

"Do you have to be so stuffy?" Malleson asked, with an unexpected grin.

"Yes," said Justin. "I do, over this."

"Then it's about your cousins."

"It could concern them."

"And you are too loyal to them to talk freely," said Malleson dryly.

"If it has to be official—yes."

Malleson lifted his fork slowly, then spoke through a burst of laughter from the tennis courts.

"Supposing we try it this way," he said. "I will keep it confidential—no report, no talking to anyone—unless it seems to me a matter for the police. If it isn't, then of course I can advise as a friend but not as a police officer."

Justin's mood eased. "Do you have to be so stuffy?" he demanded.

Malleson chuckled.

Justin told him exactly what had happened, from the moment he had found the dog on the porch to the moment when he had found the sparrow and talked to Bertha. He ate very little as he talked but Malleson ate steadily, watching intently all the time. It was impossible to guess what was passing through his mind. Every now and again he nodded understanding of a point, and the moment Justin finished, he said:

"Did you recognize either of the dogs?"

"No."

"You say you decided to bury the first only after finding the second at your house?"

"That's right."

"I suppose I can understand it," said Malleson. "The second one proved it wasn't an accident. Now, you think it's Maurice or one of the others. Early today you wanted to make as little fuss as possible, but after this latest incident—the bird—you feel driven to find out for certain whether one of your cousins is behind it. Am I about right?"

"Very much so."

"I'm not sure that any indictable crime has been committed," Malleson said judicially. "It depends on how the dogs were killed, whether they were stolen, whether there was any cruelty." He paused, finished the last piece of crust on his plate, and went on, "So you want my advice, Justin?"

"I'll be very grateful for it."

"Very well," said Malleson. "Let me treat this officially—make a report and detail an officer to find out what is going on. It shouldn't be difficult to find out how the dogs were killed and how they got where they did. Once we know, we can decide what action to take. Now don't answer at once," he went on, almost sharply. "Eat in silence for a few minutes and listen to me." Slowly, Justin began to eat. "This could simply be a vicious prank. You get under the skin of a lot of people, you know. They don't realize that you're as severe on yourself as you are, sometimes, on others. I know of at least two youths who would gladly cut your throat."

"*What?*" exclaimed Justin.

"You saw them trying to get into the cinema after the place was closed," said Malleson. "They were sent to a reform school for six months, and have just been released."

"Good lord! I'd forgotten!"

"*They* haven't," Malleson said dryly. "And your little habit of reporting on drunks who beat their wives doesn't endear you to the husbands, you know."

"Habit!" echoed Justin. "*Twice*, at the most, and only because the wives asked me to help them as *they* daren't report their husbands."

"I'm not saying whether I think you're right or wrong," Malleson said. "I am telling you that when you do what you conceive to be your duty as a citizen you can get under the skin of quite a lot of people. You know the truth about you, Justin, don't you?"

Justin put down his knife and fork. "No. What *is* the truth?"

"You take it for granted that decent behavior, goodness if you like, should be common to all. Well, it isn't. There's a lot of evil and there's a lot of beastliness, and some people who look clean and wholesome outside are cesspools within. You don't live in the world as it is, you live in the world as you think it should be, and a lot of people can't live up to that standard."

Very slowly, Justin finished a mouthful of his lunch.

"You know the truth about you, don't you?" he asked. "You're so used to rubbing shoulders with criminals that you don't realize how much good there is."

"All right," said Malleson. "You've made your point and there may be something in it, but I mix with the noncriminal, the ordinary citizen, even the do-gooders, much more than you mix with the criminal type. At least you must admit I know more about both sides than you do."

Heavily, Justin said, "All right, all right, I admit it."

"And I'm much more objective than you," went on Malleson, warming to his theme. "You take it for granted that Maurice is behind this. I don't. I don't hold any brief for Maurice. Between you and me and across this table, I think he's quite capable of it, but I doubt if he'd be fool enough to do it, or put anyone else up to doing it, unless he could be absolutely sure he wouldn't be found out. It's a pity you accused him when you did."

"Why?" demanded Justin, stung.

"Because the open confrontation you believe in, the 'look-me-in-the-eye-and-tell-me-the-truth' attitude doesn't work as often as you'd like it to. As things are, if I make inquiries and Maurice discovers we had lunch together he'll take it for granted you've put us on to him. That isn't going to improve the family relationship." When Justin didn't answer, Malleson went on in a softer tone, "I don't have to take any action that Maurice need know about. I can check the people who have their knife in you, and find out what they were doing last night and this morning—and worry you only at the office if I find anything to suggest that one of them was involved."

Into the following silence, the waitress came up and took their plates away.

"There's trifle, or ice cream, or rice pudding—that looks very nice today," she said.

"Cheese," said Malleson.

"Cheese for me, too," said Justin.

"And black coffee?"

"Please."

"Please."

Justin looked about and saw at least a dozen people he knew, some of them clients, three of them at least as much friends of Maurice as of his. One glanced across and raised a hand in greeting. Justin nodded and smiled, then looked back at Malleson.

"I shall tell Maurice and the others what's happened, and that I've asked you to investigate," he said. "If Maurice decides that I'm deliberately doing it to prove him guilty, it can't be helped. I simply have to know who did these things."

"Yes," Malleson agreed. "If you must know, this is the only way you could handle it." Maude came up with the cheese board and biscuits, and left them to help themselves. "If I've talked out of turn, I'm sorry. You're the most devastatingly honest man I've ever met, Justin, and I'd hate to see you hurt because of it."

He bent his gaze to the board, concentrating his attention on cutting into a piece of red Cheshire.

Justin returned to the office at half-past two. He needed only five minutes to walk to the museum, where the committee meeting was to be held at five o'clock, so he had good time. Maurice's door was open, which meant he wasn't back yet. He put a note on the desk—"Can we have a brief partners' meeting at three-thirty?"—and went upstairs. Both Alan and Hugo were in.

"Can do," Alan said. "I want to be off sharp at four, though. Business!" He grinned, and then his expression changed. "Have you come around to our way of thinking about Mrs. Pantanelli?"

"No," Justin said simply.

Alan said, with a sudden revival of bitterness, "You're a selfish, bloody fool! If you were a married man with three children you'd know how important this is!"

"I know how important it is," Justin said. "If we concentrate more on the business you'd have all the money you need."

"And you'd still have your precious clear conscience," Alan sneered.

Hugo, his handsome profile clear-cut against the light, sat at his desk, dictating into a tape machine. He switched it off and, as he saw Justin, stood up. He could be extremely charming, and it was easy to forget how two-faced he was by nature. He rounded the desk.

"Justin, just the chap I wanted! Shut the door, old man. . . . Justin, I want you to know I thought Maurice went a damned sight too far yesterday. I'm with him over this Mrs. Pantanelli business, God knows I need—we need—the money, but if you really can't bring yourself to do it, well, that's no reason for going on as Maurice did. And I told him so last night."

Justin, remembering how Hugo and Alan had talked that morning, said dryly:

"I'm glad you don't want to cut me down to size, too. I'd like to have a word with all of you at half-past three."

"That suits me, old chap," Hugo said. "It will give us another chance to change your mind!" His smile was infectious, and Justin's spirits lifted. He turned away as Hugo's voice rose. "Hey, did you hear about the burglary at Freeman and

Ross's place last night?" Freeman and Ross were the solicitors who did most of the firm's work.

Justin turned quickly. "No. Was anything stolen?"

"Can't get a word out of anybody, you know how taciturn old Freeman is. Malleson's not much better. He was at the offices most of the morning. All kind of rumors are floating around—half the skeletons in Hodenham are locked up in that cupboard!"

"Yes, I know," Justin said.

He was wondering why Eric Malleson had not said a word to him about it; surely that had been overdoing official reticence. He went to his office, signed letters, checked that the particulars of Corkscrew Cottage were ready off the duplicating machine and the key available, then looked through the minutes of the last meeting of the museum committee. As he finished, his door opened.

"What's the royal command about?" demanded Maurice brusquely. "I've a three-thirty appointment, and I don't want to miss it. Everyone's here now. Why not get it over?"

"No reason at all," Justin said. He could not understand Maurice's manner; it was too aggressive, as if something was worrying him—and it would not be his conscience. "No need to use the board room, either. Let's go into Alan's office." That was the handiest for all the partners, and they were soon grouped together in the room, which overlooked the back garden. "Maurice knows a little about this," Justin began. "The body of a dog was left on the porch here last night, another outside my flat, and a dead sparrow was put on my desk this morning. I thought Maurice was being unpleasant, but he says he knows nothing about it—so I've asked Eric Malleson to investigate. I'd like to know who else is after my blood."

Alan said, "I must say I don't blame you."

Hugo said, "Some practical joker—do you really want to make a fuss?"

Maurice said, "So that's your little game! I suppose you hope to prove it's me, and put me in jail for it. You make me sick."

He turned on his heel and went out.

Justin sat at his desk, fighting against a wave of hopelessness, bitterness, resentment. He felt as if there was no way of avoiding this conflict, and that it would get worse; and he could not see how it would end.

His telephone rang and he answered it.

"Mr. Justin, there's a gentleman on the line, a Mr. Smethwick, who would like to see you at his house this afternoon. He's been called abroad, he says, and wants to put the house on the market."

Justin caught his breath.

"No," he said. "I can't go out now, Bertha. Mr. Alan or Mr. Hugo can go. Tell him I'm very sorry I can't."

He meant, of course, that he wouldn't; he couldn't face clients in this mood. It would be all he could do to be ready for the museum committee.

Chapter 7

SECOND MEETING

JUSTIN WAS five minutes late for the museum committee meeting, and once there found it hard to concentrate. In the oak-paneled room of a sixteenth-century house converted into a museum fifty years ago there was general business about new exhibits, special exhibitions, cooperation with the Hodenham Art College, and—as always—the problem of funds. Justin slipped into an uneasy reverie, and suddenly heard the chairman say:

"Can you help us, Justin?"

"What's that?" asked Justin, startled. "I'm sorry, I didn't hear . . ."

"We were talking of the possibility of getting gifts of covenant," the chairman said.

They were always talking of getting such gifts, by which they could profit considerably.

"I don't know of anyone else we might approach," Justin said.

"You were having forty winks," a young committee woman remarked, and provoked a general chuckle. "We wondered whether we could persuade any of the people who've left us something in their wills to make the gift in advance, through covenants."

"I know I'm new on this committee, but what *is* a covenant?" asked an attractive girl with youthful-looking, windswept hair.

"If you covenant to give so much a year for seven years, the museum can reclaim the tax you pay on the amount donated—

it's rather complicated but it's very helpful," explained the chairman. "As a matter of fact, Justin, I wondered if you could prevail on Mrs. Pantanelli to make such a gesture. We so urgently need money if we are to maintain the standard of our collection." (Everyone was after Mrs. Pantanelli's money.)

"I don't think it's very likely," Justin said.

"Will you try?" a man insisted.

It was impossible to ask Mrs. Pantanelli; the obvious answer and the one that sprang to Justin's lips was "No, I don't think I should." Normally, he would have said so. But the onslaught from Maurice had affected him, and some of the things Malleson had said had disturbed him deeply. So he answered in a rare mood of compromise:

"If I get an opportunity, yes."

"Everyone knows that she will eat out of your hand," a man said officiously.

Justin felt a sudden flash of anger, fought it back, forced a smile at the general chuckle that followed, saw the chairman looking at him with unusual concentration, and wondered whether he had revealed his anger. The chairman, James Tomlinson, was a man whom he had known for many years yet had never known well. A once highly placed barrister, he had lived in the district a long time. He had had a coronary several years previously, retired from the bench, and concentrated on social and community work, which he could do without pressure. He was a tall, nearly bald man with faintly blue lips, a sure sign of heart trouble. He had a quiet yet impressive voice and always managed to convey an impression of self-importance.

"The next item on the agenda is that of special exhibits," he said. "Has anyone any suggestions?"

Someone suggested some Roman pottery, recently dug up in a neighboring town; the girl with the wind-swept hair knew a man who collected Aztec jewelry, and promised to approach him.

"Excellent, excellent," said Tomlinson. "Has anyone else any proposals? . . . No? . . . Then I have one which I hope will be of interest. I met an old friend last week, a Dr. Cellini, and discovered that he has three *superb* pieces of Cellini's wrought gold—quite beautiful and extremely valuable—as well as some smaller pieces of gold and silver work of the Italian Renaissance period. He would be happy for us to exhibit these for a week or two, subject to proper and sufficient insurance, of course, at any time. We have a gap at the beginning of October . . ."

The name Dr. Cellini was familiar, and Justin wondered where he had heard it before. As the meeting broke up a little group formed around the chairman, and a short, smug man asked:

"Is this Dr. Cellini a psychiatrist?"

"That he is," agreed Tomlinson.

"I was in court one day and heard him give evidence on behalf of a man accused of murder. He was very impressive, I must say," the committee man volunteered. "Nothing to look at, but *very* impressive as a witness."

Justin vaguely remembered reading about the case.

"Wasn't that the man who defended the boy who killed his mother?" asked a waspish little woman in a gray, masculine-type suit. "I remember the case well."

"They let murderers off far too lightly these days," remarked a big man with a lisping voice. "They should bring back the rope, that's what I say. A man doesn't deserve to live once he's killed someone."

"That's right, Dick," said a thin man with a leathery face. "Let's all go back to justice, cave-man style."

Justin went off with Peggy Nelson, the girl with the windswept hair, who lived near the office and whom he had known as a little girl. She looked about eighteen but was, in fact, in her middle twenties. As he started off, she said:

"Are you all right, Justin?"

"I'm fine, thanks."

"You look rather pensive."

"Well, that is how I feel, actually."

"Anything Auntie Peggy can help with?"

Justin laughed. "No, I don't think so."

"I'd love to if I can!"

"I know you would," Justin said, and glanced at her. She flushed slightly and turned away. "And I'd call on you if there were anything you could do."

He was saved from the need to say anything further by a sudden rush of traffic. He pulled up at the end of the street where Peggy lived, and stretched across to open the door for her. Quite deliberately, she leaned forward, a little nearer than convention demanded.

"It isn't good to be on your own as much as you are," she said. "I might be able to help more than you think, Justin." She got out of the car, her eyes glistening mischievously, blew him a kiss, and walked off. She had very shapely, slender legs.

"Well I'm damned!" Justin exclaimed, and then turned a corner onto the roundabout.

Outside the offices of Mendelson and Gray stood an empty police car. Justin turned the next corner, parked, and walked back to the office. It was nearly six o'clock, and only Bertha was in the outer office, sealing some letters. The moment she saw him she jumped up.

"Oh, I *am* glad you're back, Mr. Justin! No one else is here and I didn't know what to do, so I said they could do what they wanted—the *police*, I mean. They're digging in the garden for something. I do hope I was right." There was no indignation in her manner now, only anxiety.

"Of course you were right," Justin said. "I'll go and see what they're up to. Are there any messages?"

"Mr. Eccles telephoned and said he would like to buy 51 Cemetery Drive, and he's putting the deposit check in the mail."

"That's good!"

"Mr. Hugo said he won't be in tomorrow," Bertha went on.

"I see."

"There's nothing else of importance. I'm just going to the mailbox, and I'll be back to tidy up."

"I'll see you then," said Justin.

He went along the passage, opened the unlocked back door, and saw two policemen digging at the spot where he had buried the dogs. Two canvas sacks were at one side—the bodies obviously in them. Farther along the garden Eric Malleson was moving about, as if looking for something in or on the ground.

Justin nodded to the policemen and joined Malleson, who looked up, unsurprised.

"We're taking the exhibits away," he announced. "I want to find out how they were killed."

"I would like to know that, too. What else do you expect to find here?" asked Justin.

"I'm just checking," Malleson answered, with a half smile. "Do you object?"

"Naturally not, though I can't say I see the point of it," replied Justin. Abruptly, he added, "Why didn't you tell me about the burglary at Freeman and Ross?"

"Why should I?" asked Malleson evenly.

"It was hardly confidential—it was bound to be all over the town. They do a lot of work for us, and some of our documents might have been affected."

Malleson's gaze didn't falter. "I didn't know then whether anything of yours was missing."

"You could have mentioned it in passing, surely."

Malleson hesitated, then smiled with unexpected warmth. "Yes, I could. I could also say I didn't want to worry you more than you were worried already, but I'll take a leaf out of your book and be brutally frank. I wanted to get the reaction of your cousins before talking to you about it. If it comforts you, your reaction is completely normal. So is Alan's. Hugo has gone off somewhere and won't be back until tomorrow, and from all I hear Maurice is in a very jumpy mood." Malleson put up a hand, palm outward. "Don't say you didn't ask for it!"

"Are you saying you think one of *us* knows something about the burglary?"

"I'm saying that I want to know of anyone who is nervous because of the burglary. Maurice may be, so may Hugo."

"So may a dozen people in Hodenham!"

"I could name some of them, but I won't," Malleson said dryly. "I've made a statement to the press, so there's no reason why you shouldn't know now. Nothing valuable appears to have been stolen. A number of deed boxes were opened and their contents disturbed. Two flash bulbs were found in a wastepaper basket, and suggest that some of the documents might have been photographed. And if you want me to go on from there, I can tell you that quite a number of documents at Freeman and Ross were highly personal to certain people, and could give any unscrupulous individuals an opportunity for blackmail."

Heavily, Justin said, "So a lot of people really *have* cause for alarm."

"Yes."

"Have you any grounds for suspecting Maurice and Hugo might be among them?"

"No," Malleson answered. "You're more likely to know whether they have any skeletons in their cupboard." He glanced up as one of the policemen approached. "All through, Sims?"

"Yes, sir. We've been down six feet, and the last three obviously haven't been disturbed for years. There are signs of water at five and a half feet, wouldn't have to dig far to avoid paying your water rate here, sir!"

"All right, fill the hole in and take the corpses to the laboratory. Dr. Price is expecting them." Malleson nodded dismissal, then lowered his voice. "Justin, I had to make sure nothing else was buried beneath those dogs. Now I *am* sure."

"What on earth could you expect to find?"

"When you survey a property you don't expect to find anything wrong, you simply check to make sure everything's all right—no damp, no structural weakness, no woodworm, no dry rot. That's all I'm doing. Checking."

"I wish I knew what you were checking for," Justin said slowly.

"Dirt," Malleson answered cryptically.

While Justin was staring at him, and the garden seemed still and silent, there was a movement at the back door, and Justin glanced around to see Charlotte Warwick standing there.

It was after six—and he had forgotten her.

Chapter 8

CORKSCREW COTTAGE

CHARLOTTE SAW the police filling in the hole, the sacks, the spades—everything, as she approached Justin. Malleson was watching with obvious interest, but the two policemen pretended to notice nothing.

"Charlotte!"

"Justin, what's going *on?*"

"May I tell you later?"

"Yes, of course, but—"

"I'd like you to meet a friend of mine," said Justin. "Inspector Eric Malleson, of the Criminal Investigation Department. Eric—I mentioned Mrs. Warwick, didn't I?"

"Yes indeed," Malleson said. "You were here last night when the first of the dogs—"

"*First?* Were there more?" Charlotte was aghast.

"It has developed into a major mystery," Justin said dryly. Until Charlotte had arrived he had been inwardly tense, even antagonistic, but now that she was here he felt much calmer. She looked delightful in a beautifully cut suit of russet brown trimmed with dark green, her serenity barely touched by concern. "I'll tell you all about it if you really want to know."

"Of course I want to know!"

"I'll be on my way," Malleson said. "Good night, Mrs. Warwick. I'll see you tomorrow, Justin, after the autopsy. No, I can go through the alley, don't worry about me."

As they followed him, walking more slowly, Bertha appeared at the back door, obviously agitated, as obviously vexed that she had come too late.

"What on earth are they digging for, Mr. Justin?"

Justin briefly outlined what had happened, then changed the subject.

"I'm going to take Mrs. Warwick out to see Corkscrew Cottage, Bertha. The keys are still on my desk, aren't they?"

"Yes, just where you left them." Bertha hesitated, and then went on huskily, "I'm sorry I said what I did this afternoon, Mr. Justin. I really am."

"All richly deserved!" Justin reassured her. "Now you trot along home, and I'll lock up."

"No, please, I'd rather lock up as usual," Bertha pleaded. "Especially tonight, after that burglary at Freeman and—" She broke off, and for a moment looked horror-struck. "Oh, I didn't mean that I don't trust *you*, Mr. Justin! It's just that for my own satisfaction—" She broke off in confusion.

Justin put a hand on her shoulder.

"I'd rather trust you to lock up than trust myself," he told her. "I'll go and get the cottage keys." He put out a hand for Charlotte to precede him into the building, and was at the foot of the stairs when he suddenly remembered the bird that had been on his desk after lunch. He checked himself, then held Charlotte back.

"I'll go first," he said.

She looked at him curiously, but stood aside. He hurried up, almost breathless from anxiety, and strode into his room.

The desk was empty except for the usual trays, the telephones, the copy of the particulars of Corkscrew Cottage, and the keys. He was absurdly relieved, but almost immediately tensed up again, expecting Charlotte to ask what was the matter. She didn't, but glanced out of the window, saying:

"How far away *is* Corkscrew Cottage?"

"About two miles." Justin handed her the details. "How does that sound?"

She took the paper and almost at once her eyes began to

sparkle. " 'Circular staircase,' " she read out. " 'Seventeenth-century oak beams, twentieth-century plumbing.' It sounds charming."

"It *is* charming," said Justin. "Let's go!"

All tension and half fears left him as he followed Charlotte downstairs. Bertha, checking postage stamps, looked up with a smile.

"You won't be long, Bertha, will you?"

"Only a few minutes, Mr. Justin. Good night, Mrs. Warwick. I do hope you like Corkscrew Cottage."

Outside, Charlotte said, "She seems nice."

"She was my father's secretary, and knows more about the business than any of the partners." Justin saw the police car, still there, and the small boys who had been present the previous evening showing a lot of interest in the searchlight and the police sign. Nearby, at least a dozen people hovered. Outside the newspaper and bookshop, a youth called:

"Hodenham robbery—latest."

As they settled into Justin's car, Charlotte said, "I didn't realize that a London suburb would be so like a village."

"London's just a collection of villages," Justin remarked lightly. "This is one of the nicer ones, although its calm has been disturbed in the last day or two. Let's forget it, shall we?"

"Of course. Tell me more about Corkscrew Cottage."

"It's been on the market for only a couple of days," Justin answered. "The last owners had to move to the Midlands at short notice, and they left it furnished."

"Furnished!" exclaimed Charlotte.

"Most of the furniture's been removed now. You can buy what's left if it appeals to you," Justin went on. "The tenant left last week, and the owners decided to sell. We're the sole agents."

He turned off the main road, passed a modern school that seemed to spread over an enormous acreage, then some pleasant houses that stood back from the road. Suddenly the road narrowed, and on the right, with an open lawn in front of it and flower beds filled with antirrhinum, stock, daisies, and marigolds, was Corkscrew Cottage. It was tiny; the roof sloped; the windows were uneven; one side wall was no more than four feet from the ground.

"It's just like a corkscrew!" Charlotte cried.

"Our descriptions never lie," Justin said. He pulled up into a wide approach, and got out to open the five-barred gate. Beyond, straight along a gravel drive, was a garage, with ramblers in full bloom covering one side, an entrance to the cottage on the other; there was a glimpse of a beech hedge, and more lawns. They got out, Charlotte approaching slowly, as if she could not believe her eyes. The night scents were not yet strong, but there was the perfume of flowers and the sweet scent of newly cut grass from a garden nearby, from which this house was separated by a hedge of Russian vine, its white flowers spreading like a carpet of snow. There was just room to pass between the hedge and the low wall—and in the wall was a tiny window.

Charlotte peered in.

"That's a store cupboard," Justin told her. "To get in there you have to be a dwarf."

They passed the window and stepped into the back garden. On one side rose trees were set in freshly turned beds; on the other, vegetables were growing sturdily—peas and runner beans, carrots, lettuce, under glass some tomato plants, a few already showing red. The side of the garage now visible had a huge rambler spreading, white and pale pink. At the far end of the garage was a small wooden tool shed.

"It's idyllic," Charlotte said very quietly. "I can't believe I could have such a stroke of luck."

"You'd better see the inside first," Justin advised. "I've the front door key."

As they strolled to the front door, the humming of bees was

loud and persistent. He pushed aside a scarlet rambler, opened the door, and stepped inside.

It was like stepping into a power house.

The humming was a high-pitched roar as bees swarmed over the hall, the circular staircase, and the doorway leading into the living room. They flew against his face and settled on his hands and arms; he felt a sharp sting on his cheek just beneath his right eye.

"Get back!" he shouted. "Back!"

He pushed backward, bumping into Charlotte, heard her exclaim; swept bees away from his hair and eyes, and slammed the door. The noise faded. He turned, to see Charlotte backing slowly away, one or two bees hovering about her.

"Are you all right?" he demanded harshly.

"Yes. Are . . . are you?"

"Nothing to worry about," he said in the same harsh voice. They stood staring at the cottage, and indeed it was idyllic. "They've swarmed in there today," Justin went on. "I was here yesterday and there wasn't a sign of them." He touched the sore spot on his cheek. "Is the stinger still in?"

"I can't see," she said. "There's a reddish bump, that's all. Oughtn't you to put something on it?"

"Soda," Justin said mechanically. "I know some people over there—they'll let me use their telephone. The quicker we get an apiarist here the better. If they swarm in there all night they will be the devil to get out tomorrow." He took her arm. "Sure you weren't stung?"

"I'd have felt it if I had been," she said. She looked apprehensive, though, and pale.

A curly-haired man mowing his lawn stopped as they reached his gate, wiped his forehead with the back of his hand, and said:

"Hello, Mr. Gray. What's the matter with your eye?"

"A bee sting, that's all," Justin answered.

"Bee stings can be very nasty—my wife's sister nearly died

from one," the man said earnestly. "I've got just the stuff. My wife bought a bottle in reserve, just in case."

"If I can use your telephone first—"

"You don't want to leave *that* any longer without attention," the man said. "Is the message urgent?"

"Corkscrew Cottage is swarming," Justin told him. He could feel his cheek throbbing, and already his eye was puffing up. "I was going to show Mrs. Warwick over it—Mrs. Warwick, Mr. Johnson."

"How do you do?"

"What's the matter?" a pleasant middle-aged woman called. "I—oh! Mr. Gray, your *eye!*"

"Better?" asked Johnson.

"Much, thanks," said Justin.

"I told you that stuff's wonderful if you get it on in time."

"Your wife did the trick by taking out the stinger."

"Oh, she's good at first aid. I called Dick Kingsley and he's coming right away. Says it's better to get them out before sunset, if he can."

"I'd heard something like that," Justin remarked.

It was ungrateful, but he wished Johnson would leave him alone with Charlotte. The sting *was* much less painful and the swelling had gone down, but his head ached, and above everything else, he wanted to think. The first reaction after he had seen the bees was simple: they had been put there or lured there.

Was that possible?

"If you don't mind I'll go and see how Kingsley handles them," said Johnson. "He's got a great net over his face, so he's not taking any chances. Brought a hive, too. Amazing, he says they'll follow the queen if you can once get her out."

"Go by all means," Justin said, trying not to sound too eager.

"Stay here as long as you like, won't you?"

"You're very kind."

When Johnson had gone from the small, pleasant room, there was silence except for a distant lawnmower, a car, somewhere not far off, a baby crying. Charlotte sat in a window seat, overlooking the garden, Justin in an armchair.

"There's quite a crowd," Charlotte remarked. She still looked pale and uneasy.

"It must have been a shock."

"Yes . . . and for you."

She looked at him levelly.

"Justin, do you think they were put there deliberately?" There was no hint of drama in her voice, just plain matter-of-factness, with a hint of uncertainty.

"They could have been." He was as matter-of-fact as she.

"As part of this campaign against you, I mean."

"Campaign?"

"Well, it *is* one, isn't it?"

"It looks like it," Justin admitted reluctantly.

"Would you care to talk about it?"

Justin hesitated before he said, "I think so, but not here. I wondered if you would care to have a light meal at my flat. We could talk there."

She hesitated, and he thought she was going to find an excuse, but then she said simply:

"I'd love to."

Again, Justin was surprised at his deep pleasure, almost excitement.

"Shall we wait to see if the cottage is cleared of the bees before it's dark?" he suggested.

"Would you like to?"

"Yes, I think so."

Five minutes later they walked across to the cottage. A very short, thin man wearing enormous gloves and a net hood over his head, was standing in the middle of the front lawn. Bees swarmed around him, and more hummed incessantly about the entrance to the hive. A tiny woman, gloved but not hooded, came out of the cottage, calling:

"There aren't many left, just the odd one or two." She recognized Justin. "It's a lucky thing we got here so quickly, Mr. Gray. If they'd really settled you would have had a terrible job. I've known bees to spend a whole summer in an empty house, and it doesn't seem to matter what you do, you can't get rid of them. Are you going in?"

"Just for a few minutes, I think," Justin said.

"What caused them to swarm in there?" asked Charlotte, sounding casual.

"There were some lads playing about here this afternoon, I'm told. I'll bet one of the little devils caught the queen and pushed her through an open window," the woman said. "I've known it to happen before. Some of these lads don't know the meaning of fear, I will say that for them!"

"So it was done deliberately," Charlotte said in a low-pitched voice.

Justin gripped her arm to silence her. The little woman, sensing mystery, glanced from one to the other, and then hurried off, saying:

"I must see if my husband needs any help."

"Let's go in," Justin said, and they stepped over the threshold.

Chapter 9

CONFIDENCES

THE EVENING SUN still shone brightly outside, but it was gloomy in the cottage. Curtains, half-drawn, shrouded the small, deep-set windows. The main room on the ground floor was quite large, only the low ceilings and oak beams made it seem cramped. Justin went across and drew a curtain farther back.

Charlotte stood in the middle of the room.

"It's unbelievable," she said. "I love every corner of it."

They went into a narrow passage; on one side was a tiny cloakroom, on the other a kitchen, fully modernized; the storeroom, more like a low-level cupboard, led off that. Standing by the stainless-steel sink, Charlotte looked over the back garden.

"Upstairs?" asked Justin.

"Yes, please, before it gets too dark."

Both of them had to lower their heads to get up the twisting staircase, where dark treads and the near-black handrail held the dull luster of centuries of polishing. The bathroom was small but adequate, the second bedroom little more than a box room, but the main bedroom, overlooking the front garden, was unexpectedly large. A four-poster bed stood against one wall; beyond it, the ceiling sloped sharply to a long, narrow window. The wide, uneven boards were bare, shiny in some places, dull where rugs and furniture had stood.

They crossed to the window.

Dick Kingsley was taking off his hood, satisfied that the bees were back where they should be. A dozen people were on the lawn, among them several small boys chasing around with no apparent purpose.

"Justin," Charlotte said quietly.

"Yes?"

"Why are they doing these things to you?"

"I . . . I'm not sure why."

"That's a strange remark," Charlotte said, looking at him straightly. They were still close to the window, and noise from the crowd filtered through to them.

"I don't know who is at the back of it," Justin said. "I know who it might be. If I'm right, then I know why."

After a pause, she asked, "Would you like to tell me who you suspect?"

"My cousin Maurice," Justin said, marveling that he felt he could confide in this girl, who was, after all, almost a stranger. "Perhaps all three of my partners, working together."

"Why on earth *should* they?" Charlotte sounded aghast.

"They want to arrange a business deal that isn't . . . isn't straight."

"I *see*. And they need your help?"

"That's it."

After another pause, Charlotte asked quietly, "Is it a *very* crooked deal?"

"I think it is."

"And once you think a deal is crooked you won't have anything to do with it?"

"Would you?" Justin countered.

"I might," Charlotte answered quietly. "It would depend on the circumstances."

"Surely not," protested Justin. "Either a thing's right, or it's wrong."

"Black or white?" she asked. "No gray at all?"

"People can be gray," Justin answered. "We excuse ourselves for doing what we shouldn't because other people would do it, or no one would find out, or it's not illegal, only wrong." There was bitterness in his voice. "Surely *you* can't argue that it's right to do what you know you shouldn't."

"You must be a difficult man to work with in today's world," Charlotte remarked, almost sharply.

"Probably," Justin conceded, wondering how they had come to this mood of discussion. "I don't much like today's world."

"You have to live in it," she replied. "Don't you *ever* compromise?"

"Not if a thing appears to me to be wrong," Justin answered, and every word seemed to have an echo: *Humbug, humbug, humbug, smug, smug humbug.*

"Not even in business?" Charlotte persisted.

"Not even in business," asserted Justin doggedly. He felt an unusual tension, and a feeling of acute disappointment in Charlotte. He had thought she would see things much as he saw them, would accept his standards, but obviously she thought much as the others did. "Last night . . ." He paused.

"Yes?"

"You made a certain criticism of England."

"Did it hurt you?" she asked very quietly.

"No," he said. "It didn't hurt in the slightest. The fact that you were justified, hurt—the fact that so many things have gone wrong in England hurt very much. But you"—he gave a short laugh—"you were so frank in criticism that I thought you were—" He broke off, suddenly embarrassed, staring at her. In this soft light she looked very beautiful, and there was a glow in her eyes that seemed to touch them with gold. Her lips were slightly parted too, as if in anxiety. She didn't prompt him, so at last he went on, "I thought you would be honest in all things."

"No," she said. "No, I'm not as honest as that. I accept the world as it is."

"I don't. I *can't*." He felt he had to justify himself.

"Surely you're not trying to change the world!"

"The world is made up of individuals," Justin said simply. "If a sufficient number hold certain standards, those are accepted." When she didn't answer at once, he continued, "you look exactly like my cousins when I'm telling them I won't cheat."

"Don't you *ever* cheat?" she wanted to know.

"Not consciously," he answered slowly. *Smug, humbug, smug, smug, smug.*

"My goodness," she said in a strained voice, "you really mean that, don't you?"

"Of course I mean it!"

"And now you're suffering for it, obviously."

"I may be," Justin said. "Or else I'm suffering because Maurice and the others have the wrong standards."

He felt the intensity of her gaze too keenly, moved again, and looked out of the window. He stiffened immediately, for a police car had pulled in behind his, and a policeman was speaking to Kingsley. The apiarist was talking very quickly, his mouth working like that of a ventriloquist's doll.

Charlotte moved to the window to see what had caught his attention.

"Why should the police come here?" she wondered.

"It was a patrol passing, I expect, checking on the crowd outside an empty house. Shall we go down now?"

"Not yet," she said. "Not yet, until you've finished telling me what this is about, Justin."

"I've told you everything that matters, and on that we don't see eye to eye." He was surprised by the measure of his disappointment, for she looked exactly as he had imagined her to be—as if there wasn't a lie or a dishonest act in her whole being. "There isn't any point in discussing it if we're looking at the same thing from different angles. I can't see it your way, you can't see it mine."

"Stiff-necked," she said briskly.

"What's that?" he asked, startled.

She gave him a broad, delightful smile, and touched his arm.

"I said you were a stiff-neck. To me, that's worse than telling an occasional lie or getting one over your competitor in a business deal. If you won't try to see the other person's point of view, how can you expect others to try to see yours?"

"But it's so obvious that I'm right!"

"Complacent, too," she said, but her light tone robbed the words of sting.

In spite of himself, Justin laughed. "The repertoire, I am told, ranges from humbug to hypocrite, from—"

"And it hurts?"

"It drives me into—" He broke off, gripped her hands, and went on in a much louder voice, "Why on earth are we talking like this?"

"Don't evade the issue," Charlotte rebuked. "You've done that too often in the past." Before he could reply, she said, "How long have you lived alone, Justin?"

He said gruffly, "Five years."

"*Much* too long to argue only with yourself!"

"Now you're talking nonsense!"

"No I'm not," Charlotte retorted firmly. "Be honest with yourself. How often do you really see any point of view but your own?"

"I bend over backward to see the other side!"

"Doesn't it ever occur to you that when you bend over backward you get a distorted view?" asked Charlotte. "Justin, listen to me—and please forgive me, I know I've no right to talk to you like this, but perhaps it's better for a stranger to say it, at least you can't impute any ulterior motive to one." She paused long enough for him to break in, and so to stop her, but when he did not she took his hands firmly, and went on, "I *do* know what I'm talking about. I tried for years to see my husband's point of view by bending over backward as you call it, and I couldn't. It wasn't until I stepped into his shoes and looked at the situation as *he* saw it that I realized how it looked to him. How *I* looked to him. And"—she drew a deep breath—"it wasn't a very pretty picture."

As she spoke she became more and more earnest, more anxious to impress him; and, he thought, she became more and more beautiful. Her grip on his hands tightened and she drew him a little closer, as if willing him to understand her. All he understood was that she meant everything she said, and that behind it there was an intensely personal story, perhaps an emotional passion, which goaded her.

Gently he said, "Charlotte, there *are* such things as ethics. There *are* some things where it isn't easy to see what's right or what's wrong. I'm not so pig-headed as you seem to think, but when you *are* sure of the right course, it's impossible to take any other. If you knew the circumstances of this particular issue, I can't believe you'd see it any differently from the way I see it. If you did—" He broke off.

She finished for him. "If I did, then obviously we wouldn't have anything in common."

He freed his hands, and raised them helplessly. "So you can read my thoughts!"

"A lot of your thoughts aren't difficult to read," she said, almost sharply. "Justin, it *isn't* simply a question of who's right and who's wrong on this particular issue—it's a question of attitudes. You *must* be able to see the other person's point of view before you can put it right if it's wrong, or put your own right if *that's* wrong. It isn't any use being stubborn."

Justin did not quite know why this word angered him so. There were a lot of contributory factors. She *was* a stranger and she was talking to him as if she had every right in the world to criticize him. She took it for granted that she was right and he was wrong. There wasn't any reason why he should allow her to talk to him like this. And since yesterday, when Maurice had flown at him, person after person seemed to be flinging criticism: Malleson, Bertha Briggs—yes, even Bertha!—the museum committee, Peggy Nelson—my God, Peggy *Nelson!*—and now Charlotte Warwick, when both last night and tonight he had exerted himself to be helpful, gone far beyond the bounds of normal business.

"I don't think we're going to get anywhere by discussing it," he said stiffly. "Would you like to look around the cottage again before we go?"

She put out a hand, appealingly. "Justin, I didn't mean—"

"Of course you didn't. The fault is mine. The root of the matter goes too far back for anyone who hasn't lived with it to understand. And now would you like another look around the cottage?"

She turned away from him slowly. He knew that she was hurt, but in this present mood he blamed her. He was surprised to see how dark it was; the only light was near the window, and it would be pointless to go from room to room again.

"No," she said. "We'd better go."

"I hadn't noticed it was getting dark so suddenly."

"No," she said, with a catch in her breath, "I hadn't either."

She led the way, gripping the handrail tightly, reached the bottom, and had the front door open before he could touch it. As he locked the door she walked across the lawn toward the car. The lock jammed, and he made a mental note to have it repaired as he fiddled this way and that with the key. His mood was changing slowly. He wished he had not taken offense, yet still justified himself for doing so. Suddenly he realized that he had asked her home for supper, and it was going to be difficult, almost embarrassing. He had taken her so much for granted that he had acted much too precipitantly— it was always a mistake. Would he be well advised to take her out to dinner? That in some ways might be less trying.

The door locked at last, he turned around. He didn't see her by the car, but assumed she was sitting waiting for him. As he drew nearer, however, he saw that the car was empty. Surely she hadn't walked off in a huff. He quickened his step and reached the gate.

She wasn't in sight.

"Oh, damn the woman!" he exclaimed aloud.

The branches of an oak tree overhung the road in one direction; she was probably just beyond that, and if he hurried he could catch up with her. He closed the gate and reversed into Field Lane, went past the oak tree, and saw no sign of her. He reversed into a driveway and went in the other direction—and saw a single-decker bus moving off from a bus stop just beyond the point where the road had narrowed.

There was no sign of Charlotte.

"And the bus goes to the station," he muttered, glancing at his watch.

It was a quarter past nine, and she would almost certainly catch the ten o'clock train. If he hurried he could get there ahead of her, but should he? She was clearly a creature of impulse. The way she had virtually attacked him out of her half— her infinitesimal!—knowledge of him and of the facts made that obvious. So did her sudden decision to walk out on him.

Should he overtake the bus? Was there any point in humbling himself?

He made a decision, suddenly, drove fast but in a long way around, and reached a lumber yard near the station and opposite the bus stop. He parked behind a lumber shed, and within two minutes heard the bus approaching. Only two or three people were inside, and at first he thought she wasn't there—but at last he saw her hurrying up the slope toward the station.

He felt an almost irresistible temptation to go after her, but fought the impulse down. She turned into the ticket office without looking back. Well, why should she look back? In the distance the roar of the train for London sounded, drawing rapidly nearer. He did not wait for it to arrive, but drove slowly back to the main part of town. He always made a point of dropping the keys into the office, in case he was delayed the next morning, and he pulled up outside the building feeling gloomy and yet still justifying his attitude. She simply had no right to talk to him as she had done.

As he reached the door he heard the telephone ringing; so late at night, it must be a wrong number, but he opened the door and went in, picked up the receiver from the front of Bertha's desk, and said:

"Justin Gray."

"Oh, thank goodness!" exclaimed Bertha. "I thought I'd never get you. I must have just missed you at Corkscrew Cottage. There's an urgent message from Mrs. Pantanelli, at least *about* Mrs. Pantanelli. Apparently she's had another stroke, and she's asking for you."

Chapter 10

MRS. PANTANELLI

BERTHA SAT by Justin's side as he drove.

"I'm sure I ought to come with you, in case there's anything I can do. . . . The doctor tried your flat *and* the office, and when there was no answer he rang me. I was just going to the dressmaking class at the Technical College . . . not that that matters in view of *this*. . . . And when I got out to Corkscrew Cottage they said you'd been hurt and had left. Oh, it was such a mess. Then I saw Mr. Kingsley and he said you'd gone back to the cottage so I went after you again. . . . I'm really too old to dash about so much on my bicycle, Mr. Justin."

He was startled into comment. "Good gracious me! Why didn't you get a taxi?"

"Well, I suppose the truth is I didn't think," confessed Bertha. "Anyhow, you'll be there in five minutes, so everything's all right."

"Did the doctor say how Mrs. Pantanelli was?"

"He said she was very gravely ill, that's all I can tell you."

Justin nodded, and his thoughts drifted back over the years he had known Louise Pantanelli. She still lived in the big old house where she had gone directly after her marriage, over fifty years ago. It stood on a wooded hill on the outskirts of Hodenham, solitary and forlorn, surrounded by row after row of small modern houses, which, compared with its dull red brick and castellated turrets, its gray slate roof and its big, sash-type windows, looked like glass and pasteboard boxes. The position was so unusual that, approaching, one could see the crisscross of pale new roads leading to and about the estate, and the wider, darker road that led past the house, which was called Hilltop.

Two cars stood on the gravel driveway near the big porch and the massive front door.

With a strange twinge, almost of pain, Justin thought of what his cousins had said about Mrs. Pantanelli. This might well be the last seizure. If she died then charities *would* get the profit on those four houses.

What the devil was the matter with him? It was *her* money, *her* will, her intention that charities should profit. Was he weakening simply because of a strange woman's strictures? *Strictures?* Her ethical casuistry was more like it.

Mrs. Pantanelli lived here alone except for an elderly couple, servants for half a century, the woman the housekeeper, the man gardener and general factotum. Justin knew them well, but had never particularly liked them. The man, Carmichael, opened the door before Justin rang. He was massive and florid, looking much less than his seventy-odd years.

"Good evening, Mr. Gray. I am very glad you have arrived."

"I came as soon as I had the message," Justin said. "How is she?"

"I think she's just holding on, sir, until she's had a word with you."

"Is this one of her lucid spells?"

"As lucid as she's been for months, sir."

"Is Dr. Nash with her?"

"Yes, sir—and the nurse."

Justin nodded, and turned to Bertha. "If I haven't come down for you in fifteen minutes, you go home," he said. "Call Miss Briggs a taxi if she wants one, Carmichael, will you?"

"Yes, sir."

Justin made his way up the big mahogany staircase, which had a half-landing three-quarters of the way up. The only light came from a crystal chandelier, with at least twenty lights on it, hanging from the ceiling of the big, square hall. At the landing was a stained-glass window bearing two coats of arms. The banisters gleamed; oil portraits seemed to emerge from the shadows. The wallpaper was dark, giving the whole place a somber look. At the head of the stairs was a wide gallery, which had two turns in it; all the rooms on this floor led off the gallery.

Louise Pantanelli's room was halfway along the first passage; one could step out of it, cross the gallery in two strides, and look down into the hall. Now the door was ajar, and Justin pushed it slowly. The sound of stertorous breathing came, startlingly clear. The room was very large and had a high ceiling, the walls and ceiling pale, the carpet pale, the large brass-posted bed against the wall opposite the door covered with a pale yellow bedspread.

Louise Pantanelli lay propped up on pillows. She looked so very frail. She looked so very near to death.

Dr. Nash, tall, balding, middle-aged, and paunchy, moved away from the bed. An elderly nurse in a white uniform approached Justin and spoke to him quietly.

"Mrs. Pantanelli has been asking for you. She will be glad you've come, sir."

"Never known such a stubborn old soul," remarked Nash in Justin's ear.

Stubborn. . . . In spite of the circumstances Justin had a swift mental picture of the moment in the cottage when he had become angry with Charlotte.

"What would you like me to do?" Justin asked.

"Go and speak to her," said Nash. "I don't know what she's trying to say. She seems—"

The old woman on the bed spoke in a strangely croaking voice; not deep, not harsh, but rather brittle. The words were quite clear, and uttered very slowly.

"I wish to see Justin Gray. He is the only man I can trust."

"That's what I was trying to tell you," Nash said. "Go on."

Justin whispered, "Send for Bertha Briggs, she's downstairs." He moved toward the bed and stood looking down. The cheeks and eyes of the woman lying there were sunken; the thin, parchment-colored lips were drawn inward. After a long pause:

"I'm here," Justin said quietly.

"Justin," she said, and her eyes opened slowly, her right hand moved on the sheet, and he took it gently in his own. "Justin," she repeated, "they are trying to rob me." Between every word there was a noticeable pause, as if she was recalling each from some dark recess in her memory.

"Who is, Mrs. Pantanelli?" Justin asked clearly.

"They are trying to rob me, Justin," she said. And as she finished Bertha appeared on the other side of the bed, her notebook in her hand.

"If they are trying to rob you, I will find them and I will stop them," promised Justin, speaking with great deliberation. "What are they trying to take, do you know?"

"They want me—they want me to sign my money away," she stated.

"Who does?" Justin asked gently.

He had almost forgotten that Bertha was now taking every word down.

The old woman might be right, of course, but this might well be a hallucination. She had always been afraid of robbery, always talked of unnamed enemies. Even in her old pre-seizure days, when her intelligence had been beyond doubt, she had suspected that friends of her late husband, her ad-

visers, even her banks and lawyers, were not trustworthy.
Even then she had often said, "You're the only one I can
trust, Justin."

"Justin," she said, "they want me to alter my will."

"Who does?" asked Justin with quiet insistence. "Please try
to tell me." He leaned closer to her and and took her other
hand. "If I know, I can stop them."

"Don't let them," she begged. "Please don't let them. Is
the doctor here?"

"Yes."

"Bring him closer, please. Is Nurse here, too?"

"Yes."

"Bring her, please," said Mrs. Pantanelli.

It was almost impossible to believe that she had ever been
non compos mentis. Certainly at this moment she knew exactly what she wanted. The others heard her and drew near,
until all three were standing close, actually touching each
other, Justin in the middle.

"We're all here," he said. "What do you want to say, Mrs.
Pantanelli?"

She opened her eyes.

"You are to be my only executor," she said clearly. "No one
else. Not the bank. Not the solicitors. Just you. And you are
to carry out *all* the conditions of my will. Do you understand,
Justin, *all* of them. It is the will I signed in April 1965, and it
is lodged with the lawyers. Jacob Freeman knows. I put it into
his hands and signed it in his presence and the presence of his
assistant. Do you understand?"

"Yes, I understand perfectly."

"Good," she said. "Good. Thank you. Thank you very
much, Justin. You"—she gave a sigh that might have been a
yawn, certainly she looked unutterably weary, and the thick,
veined lids dropped over her eyes—"you have been as a son to
me, Justin. As a son."

He felt her hands go slack. She was still breathing, but it was almost impossible to believe she would go on living for very long. Bertha moved away, a hand at her eyes; the others turned as he stood looking down on her. His mind was filled with pictures and his head with sounds—of the meeting the other day, of the pressure they had brought to bear on him, of the certainty that he had felt that he must refuse. He felt immeasurably glad that he had not yielded to them.

Bertha whispered, "I got everything, Mr. Justin."

"That's good."

"Shall I type it out tonight?"

"Wait downstairs for a little longer," Justin said. "I'll tell you then."

Obediently, she turned and left the room.

Justin saw Dr. Nash and the nurse standing by the bed again, Nash's plump forefinger on the old woman's wrist. It was impossible to judge what he was thinking, certain only that her condition was very grave. Then he saw the nurse and doctor glance at each other and it seemed to him there was something almost baleful about their expressions. The contrast was so marked, too; Nash was over-fleshy, rather red-faced, a big, buoyant man, as quiet as a boy might be in the presence of a feared master, but untidy—cigar ash on his waistcoat and lapel, tie awry, jacket and trousers rumpled. The nurse was trim, prim, angular, starched. Even the hair that showed above the starched cap looked taut and strained. She had a pallid face and rather pale gray eyes.

Nash cleared his throat with a harsh "Hurrumph!" and joined Justin.

"Only a matter of time," he remarked. "Hours, probably."

"I was afraid of that," Justin said.

"Afraid," echoed Nash. He put a hand on Justin's arm and the warmth of the palm struck through almost at once; for the first time Justin realized how stuffy the room was. "Have a word outside," Nash went on, and they stepped onto the gallery. It was warm out here, but much less close. The great hall was empty, and strangely silent. There was no sign of Bertha, nor of Carmichael.

Nash's breathing was almost as heavy as Mrs. Pantanelli's had been. He took out a small cigar and rolled it between his fingers.

"Don't know how she held on," he declared. "Desperately anxious to see you, Justin."

"She may—she may have had delusions."

"Doubt it," said Nash. "Doubt it very much. I've attended her for a long time, you know. These lucid patches were not infrequent—damn it, you know that well enough. She thought she was being robbed, but I don't think she knew she was being murdered."

He looked at Justin with a peculiar half smile, as if he wanted to add, "Aren't I a clever chap?"

Justin heard the word "murdered" and understood exactly what Nash was saying, and yet did not at first take in its full significance. He was irritated by that half smile, more like a grin, although he knew that Nash was simply enjoying his moment of revelation.

"Be serious," Justin said sharply.

"I'm deadly serious, old boy," declared Nash.

"Murdered is a—" Justin broke off.

"Yes, yes, I know. I'm telling you this in confidence, as you're the executor. Shouldn't go into details, I'll have to report it immediately to the police. Bad business."

"I find it very hard to believe," Justin said.

"You don't think I'd make such a statement if I weren't sure of my facts, do you?" Nash either was, or pretended to be, affronted. "Come, old boy—I've given you a professional opinion. Don't challenge it." When Justin didn't answer, he went on, "I know you, Justin—never really occurs to you that people are bad, does it? Wicked, some of them. Someone poisoned Mrs. Pantanelli, and I hope the police soon find out who and why."

Justin said heavily, "Will you telephone them from here?"

"I think so, yes. You don't happen to know who's on duty tonight, do you?"

"No," Justin answered. He drew in a long, slow breath, and went on, "Would it be wiser to go and see them? There's an extension to the telephone, and no way of making sure you're not overheard."

"I hadn't thought of that," Nash admitted, frowning. "I really shouldn't leave. . . . Justin! I've just had an idea. You slip into the police station and tell them what I say. Tell them I'll wait here until they come. Will you do that?"

"Yes," Justin promised heavily. "Yes."

He found Bertha drinking coffee in a small room off the hall, told Carmichael he would be back, that he was running an errand for the doctor, settled Bertha into the car, and said:

"Type those notes for me tonight, will you—and let me have several copies."

"Yes, of course, I'll be glad to. I can do them on my typewriter at home. That will save you taking me all the way back to the office. What shall I do when they're done?"

"I'll call or send for them," Justin said. "How long will you need?"

"Oh, half an hour will be plenty."

"Thanks. And if I don't often show it, I do appreciate how good you are, Bertha."

She was almost clucking with delight when he dropped her at her corner and went on to the police station. It was an old red-brick building with the familiar blue lamp over the porch; a constable, standing outside, saluted. The hall was brightly lit, and through an open door Justin saw the sergeant in the charge-room bending over the counter. He looked up.

"Hello, Mr. Gray!" The man was very tall, very lean, droll-looking.

"Hello, Sergeant. Who's on duty tonight, on the CID?"

"Pretty well everyone," said the sergeant. "Mr. Malleson's still upstairs, if you would like to see him."

"He's just the man," Justin said, but he wasn't really sure whether to be glad or sorry.

Two or three minutes later he was in Malleson's small, very tidy, very efficient-looking office, with maps of the wards in Hodenham and neighboring boroughs on the walls, three telephones and a tape recorder on the desk. Malleson's eyes were red-rimmed and tired-looking, but he was affable enough.

"Sit down, Justin. I know you wouldn't come at this hour if if weren't important. No more bodies, I trust."

"I've come from Mrs. Pantanelli's," Justin said clearly. "Listen for five minutes, will you?" He told Malleson exactly what the old woman had said, exactly what Dr. Nash had told him.

Malleson did not interrupt, but before the narration was half over he was looking sternly official, all affability gone. When Justin finished, Malleson rose abruptly.

"I'll come out with you right away." He rounded the desk, went out, calling at the door of another room, "I'm going to Hilltop, Mrs. Pantanelli's place." Halfway down the stairs he turned curtly to Justin. "Mrs. Pantanelli's will was stolen from Freeman and Ross last night. Do you know of another copy?"

Chapter 11

THE SMALL BOY

THEY WERE sitting in the back of Malleson's car, driven by a plainclothes policeman who obviously knew that Malleson was in a hurry. The orange-colored sodium lights of the town center cast a faintly lurid glow onto shop fronts, pedestrians, and a few closely embracing couples in doorways. Malleson picked up a radio-telephone set that was hooked over the back of the car, flicked it on, and said:

"Inspector Malleson here. . . . Break up some couples in High Street, they're overdoing it." He put the receiver down on a clear "Right, sir" and glanced at Justin. "So you don't know of another copy of the will?"

"No."

"Do you know what's in it?"

"She told me years ago that most of her money would go to charities."

"Didn't she say any more than that?"

"No."

"She sends for you *in extremis*, yet she hadn't given you any details, hadn't consulted you about the will you were to execute?" Malleson sounded incredulous.

Stiffly, Justin said, "No."

"Don't you think that remarkable?" Malleson demanded.

Justin felt a flare of anger, exactly the feeling he had had in Corkscrew Cottage with Charlotte Warwick. This was stronger. It seemed to send a quiver almost of pain through his arms and legs, and he clenched his hands tightly, nails digging into his palms. Malleson was being aggressively hostile.

And the inference was brutally clear: he thought that Justin was lying.

"Well? Don't you?" he demanded.

"No." Justin schooled his voice to one of calm impassivity. "A great many people prefer an executor who's had nothing to do with the preparation of their will."

"What makes you so sure?" Malleson flashed.

"Jacob Freeman said so in a lecture to Rotary a few months ago."

"Oh," said Malleson, as if the simplicity of the answer had deflated him. They turned the roundabout at the offices; the only light showing was the illuminated sign of a building society, just above the fascia and reflecting insipidly on the front windows. "I hear you found a swarm of bees in Corkscrew Cottage this evening."

"I did."

"Did you know the queen bee had been captured and put in there to lure the others inside?"

"Mrs. Kingsley suggested that might be so."

"Do you regard it as another stage in the campaign against you?" demanded Malleson.

"It could be, obviously."

"Do you think it is?" Malleson barked.

Justin sat rigidly. What right had Malleson to talk to him like this? What was in his mind? Why should he, Justin Gray, answer? He stared straight ahead, as the pale blue-white lights of the Hill estate showed up and, beyond them, yellow lights at the porch and window of Hilltop. The car turned a corner rather too sharply and threw Justin against Malleson. He straightened up as quickly as he could.

"Are you going to answer my question?" demanded Malleson.

"When you stop treating me as if I were a hostile witness, yes," Justin answered.

He was aware of Malleson staring at him, saw the strong face out of the corner of his eyes as a car passed with its headlights on. He did not understand the attitude of this man whom he had thought to be his friend, and he did not fully understand himself. His head felt as if it would split—not with pain, but with tautness. He felt overwhelmingly tired, too; all he really wanted to do was rest. The car was going uphill now, and somehow the pressure at his head seemed to grow worse.

"Let me give you a piece of advice," Malleson said. "Whatever I ask you, whatever anyone asks you, tell the truth. The simple, unembellished truth."

In a voice that hardly sounded like his own, Justin said, "I always tell the truth."

There seemed a long, pregnant pause before Malleson barked, *"Do you?"*

Malleson and Nash were together for half an hour or more, alone. Justin sat in the small, book-lined room where Bertha had been an hour before. Coffee and brandy were at his side, and his head felt less taut, but he was still baffled, edgy, and angry. There *must* be a reason for Malleson's attitude, and that *"Do you?"* had come like a bullet from a gun, saying virtually, *"You don't, you're a liar."* Why should Malleson behave like this? Why should Malleson think him a liar? *Why, why, why, why?* He sipped the brandy, then sat back and closed his eyes, outwardly calm and assured, inwardly raging. A sense of disaster hovered like a great shadow close behind him, touching his head, gripping his head. The room seemed to move, slowly at first, then faster: round and round, faster and faster, round and round. . . .

He heard shouting in his ears, opened his eyes, and saw Malleson bending over him, Dr. Nash only a step behind.

"Wake up!" Malleson was insisting. "Wake up!"

Justin tried to shrug off the detaining hand.

"I . . . I am awake."

"You were shouting."

"I was shouting?"

"Yes, Justin," Nash said quietly. "You must have been under a considerable strain today. You had a nightmare."

Justin said dully, "The whole day's been a nightmare."

Malleson seemed to speak only to Nash. "May I?"

"I see no reason why not," Nash said, and drew back.

Why not what? Justin did not understand, but became aware of Malleson standing over him, another man as well as Nash in the room, the book-lined room. Nash sat down in Mrs. Pantanelli's chair; this was the room where she and Justin had sat and talked so often. It was warm, and the lights seemed very bright—too bright, they hurt his eyes.

"Mr. Gray," Malleson asked in an aloof voice," "how often have you been to this house today?"

"Once," Justin answered, then realized that was wrong, and amended, "Twice."

"Would you like to change your mind again?" demanded Malleson.

"No. I came when I was sent for, and I'm here now. That's twice."

"You weren't here earlier, then?"

"No, I was not."

"I want you to tell me the truth, Mr. Gray."

Not Justin, but Mr. Gray, Mr. Gray, Mr. Gray. Hostile witness—what the devil was happening? There seemed no sense in this at all. Nightmares, shouting, "Mr. Gray, Mr. Gray! Tell me the *truth, truth, truth, truth!*"

Justin said, with very great care, "I am telling you the truth."

"Very well." Malleson glanced around at the other man. "Did you get that?"

Get *what?*

Nash seemed to be sitting on the edge of his chair, in vibrant expectancy.

"Now, Mr. Gray, is it true that the body of a dog was left on the porch of your office building yesterday, and another at the entrance to your flat? That a bird was put on your desk today, and that a swarm of bees was enticed into Corkscrew Cottage and was there when you went to show the cottage to an alleged client?"

Alleged?

"She was a client," Justin stated sharply.

"Very well. Are the other things true?"

"Yes—you know perfectly well that they are."

"Do you know who arranged for these things to happen?"

Justin said, with an effort, "No." But what was Malleson talking about? He knew who he, Justin, suspected; they had gone into that closely.

"Are you sure, Mr. Gray?"

Justin couldn't possibly name Maurice now; there was no certainty and there were witnesses—what was Malleson up to? Had he lost his head completely?

"Are you sure you don't know?" Malleson insisted.

"Of course I'm sure!" Justin shouted. His head was splitting, there was pain and tension in his whole body, and Malleson's face seemed to blur, then come clear, then blur again. "Why the devil do you keep calling me a liar?"

Malleson said, "All right," and stepped back. "Bring him in," he said to the other man, who went immediately to the door and opened it.

Voices sounded a long way off, and yet were very clear.

"Send him in."

"In you go."

"*What are you going to do to me?*" That was a younger, coarser voice.

"Nothing you need worry about!"

"Get a move on!"

A youth came into the room, and behind him, a uniformed policeman. The youth had long, matted hair. A sweater and faded jeans fitted his body tightly. He wore no collar or tie.

Justin knew him; he was Micky Jones, one of a large family of ne'er-do-wells in Hodenham.

Seven months earlier Justin had seen this youth, with another, attempting to break into the Bijou Cinema in Harrow Street. Justin had sent for the police, and later, at juvenile court, given evidence against them. Malleson knew this—why, Malleson had actually talked about the youths at lunchtime that day!

Malleson was standing on one side. The youth was brought into the middle of the room, and, as he saw and recognized Justin, his mouth twisted, his eyes glittered, he pointed with a blackened finger, and cried:

"That's him!"

What did he mean? What were they trying to do?

Malleson asked coldly, "Are you absolutely sure?"

"You don't expect me to forget *that* bastard, do you?" the youth sneered.

"That's enough," Malleson said. "Take him back, Officer."

The uniformed man put a hand on the youth's shoulder and made him turn around. For a moment Justin thought Jones was going to spit at him, but instead he mouthed obscenities and allowed himself to be led away.

The door closed on him.

"I must be going," Nash said, struggling up from his chair. "I'll see you in the morning, Inspector. Good night, Justin."

"All right, Sergeant," Malleson said to the other man, and suddenly Justin was alone in the room with him. Once the door closed there seemed to be a subtle change in the atmosphere: Malleson relaxed noticeably, and sat on the arm of a chair.

Justin managed to ask, "Will you tell me what this is about?"

"Will you stop pretending, and face up to the fact that you've failed," said Malleson. "We're alone now, nothing we say can go on record, and I may be able to help you. I don't know what drove you to this, I don't even know whether you're in it alone. If there are others and you will name them. . . ."

Stonily, Justin said, "What do you think I've done?"

"Justin, be sensible," Malleson urged. "Young Micky Jones has confessed to everything—the dog incidents, the sparrow incident, the bees. It had all the appearance of a campaign against you, but Jones has identified *you* as the man who paid him to do all of these things."

Justin moved forward in his chair. "But it isn't true. You must know it isn't true!"

"I've every reason to believe it is," Malleson said quietly.

"To believe that boy against *me*—"

"If he was the only witness, it would hardly be so impressive," Malleson said. "Justin, I can prove this against you up to the hilt. And I can also prove that you came and saw Mrs. Pantanelli earlier this afternoon. It isn't any use lying—and you don't make a very good liar, I will say that for you. Why did you do these things, Justin? Who are you working with, or shielding? If you tell the truth now it will save you and everyone concerned an awful lot of trouble."

Justin stood up very slowly. Malleson did not rise from the arm of his chair.

"You haven't charged me with any crime," Justin said.

"Not yet," Malleson agreed.

"Then I shall go," Justin stated.

"Justin—"

"Every word you've uttered is nonsense," Justin stated flatly. "I did not pay that youth—someone has paid him to lie. I did not come to this house this afternoon—someone is lying about that. I have to find out who it is before you go too far."

He turned and reached the door.

"Justin," said Malleson, still from the arm of his chair, "you've established such a reputation for telling the absolute truth that no doubt you think this will help you. But in court the truth is established by witnesses and by facts that cannot be disproved. Your word, your denial, won't be any use unless you can find supporting evidence. I've been collecting evidence all day, and it all points to your guilt. Stop lying to me. You've always said you lived by the truth, and only the truth will help you now."

Chapter 12

NOTHING BUT UNTRUTH

A POLICEMAN STOOD by the door. The car with the driver was still waiting for Malleson. Justin walked stiffly from the porch toward the gateway and to the Hill estate. The men watched, but no one attempted to stop him. Gradually, his stride lengthened, for the crisp night air was cold against the back of his neck and his forehead; it had been very stuffy in the house.

He hardly gave a thought to walking home; it would take twenty-five minutes, no more. He hardly gave a thought to anything, he was so confused, baffled, and angry. One question went through his mind in dull refrain: *Why didn't they believe him?* That, much more than anything else, troubled and infuriated him. He lived by the truth, made a fetish of the truth—and now a man like Malleson, who knew him so well, was convinced that he was lying. Why couldn't he think clearly? . . . Why was he so confused?

Soon he was walking mechanically. Occasionally a car passed him, but most of the time the streets were deserted. The blue light cast by street lamps turned to orange as he neared the shopping area. He passed the offices of Mendelson and Gray, only glancing at the window. *Why didn't they believe him?* He turned at last into the open gateway of the house where he lived, drew near the front door, hesitated, and drew back, remembering how he had stumbled last night.

Nothing was in the way now.

He let himself in, put on the landing light from a switch by the front door, and started up the stairs. He turned dizzy and nearly fell, grabbed the handrail, and steadied himself. Then, holding onto the rail, he went up one step at a time. At the top, when he stood still, the whole landing, doors, and staircase seemed to be moving in wild circles. His bedroom was straight ahead and the bathroom led off it. He pulled off his collar and tie and took off his jacket, dropping them as he sat on the side of the bed. *Why didn't they believe him?* And why did he feel like this?

He'd had no dinner, of course.

Charlotte. . . . Why had he turned on Charlotte like that? Why had she questioned him so remorselessly?

He lay on the bed, staring at the ceiling; a street lamp cast the shadow of a treetop on both ceiling and wall. He felt his eyes closing; he had never been so weary, so bewildered, so lost . . . so lonely.

Lonely. . . . God! How lonely he was!

Who was it who had said something about being on his own too much? Who? A pretty girl. Oh yes. Peggy. Peggy Nelson. Wicked eyes. Mischievous eyes. Lovely eyes.

He went to sleep.

There was sound—harsh, intruding sound, sound he didn't want to hear. Bang, bang, bang, bang. Why didn't it stop? He did not want to open his eyes, but gradually forced himself to. It was still dark. *Thud, thud, thud, thud.* Who on earth was it, why were they making such a din? There were voices— shouting men. Damned fools, they would wake everyone up. Who would make so much noise? Where was it coming from?

"Open the door, Gray!"

He heard the words, and knew that they came from downstairs. Someone was at the front door, banging, shouting.

"Open the door!" *Bang, bang, bang, bang.*

"Open the door!" *Thump, thump, thump, thump!*

Then there were other voices.

"Stop that noise!"

"Who are you?"

There was mumbling, words he couldn't hear, but at last there was no more shouting and banging—until suddenly there was a different sound. Footsteps on the stairs. Two or three men were approaching, and as they drew closer, one asked:

"Which is his flat?"

"Opposite the stairs."

"Gray, where are you?"

"Oh, God, I hope he's all right!"

"Why shouldn't he be?"

"Gray!" That was Malleson.

Malleson appeared in the doorway, there was no mistaking his solid figure. It was a silhouette against the landing light. Justin, hitching himself up on his pillows, saw the graying hair of his landlord, who lived downstairs, and a policeman.

"Gray! Are you all right?" Malleson put the light on and it blinded Justin, making him cover his eyes with his hand. More quietly, Malleson said, "No need to worry you any more, Mr. Henderson."

Henderson peered over Malleson's shoulder. "You're not *ill*, Mr. Gray?"

"No, no." Justin struggled to a sitting position. His head was splitting, now, and the light painfully bright.

"Thank you, Mr. Henderson," Malleson said.

"If you're sure . . ." the old man began, and then added in a tone of defiance, "They couldn't make you hear, Mr. Gray. I was afraid you were ill, that's why I let them in."

"It's perfectly all right, Mr. Henderson."

As Henderson reluctantly withdrew, Justin muttered, "Did you have to come here and cause all this disturbance?"

"Yes," said Malleson. "Why didn't you answer?"

"I was asleep."

"Did you take anything?"

"Did I . . . what?"

"Oh, don't be evasive! Did you take any drug?"

"Why should I?" Justin demanded more strongly. "What—" He broke off, for it dawned on him suddenly that Malleson had feared he had poisoned himself. "Don't be a bloody fool," he growled. "I didn't feel well, that's all."

"I see." Malleson moved farther back from the bed. "I'd like to look around your flat, Mr. Gray."

"Why?"

"I haven't a warrant, but I could get one easily enough."

"Why should you want to get a search warrant?" Justin almost screamed.

"Mrs. Pantanelli is dead," Malleson announced flatly.

That shocked Justin out of his anger and resentment, and he gave a gasping "Oh." Then after a moment his voice strengthened. "Why should you want a search warrant because of that?"

"Do you want us to get a warrant, or will you allow us to search this flat?" demanded Malleson.

There was no point in trying to stop them; the fact that he felt viciously angry toward them didn't alter the fact that they could search if they wanted to. In that moment it hardly seemed to matter why.

"Do what you like," he growled.

Malleson turned away, but a policeman stood in the open door watching Justin—clearly there to make sure that he didn't destroy anything. If only they had the sense to realize that he hadn't the strength to do anything, that he could hardly get off the bed.

How long were they likely to stay?

He was not worried about what they were doing, only by the fact that while they were here he couldn't get off to sleep again. He could hear them moving about; twice it sounded as if they were shifting furniture. His eyes were so heavy he began to close them again.

Then a man called in a voice sharp with triumph, "Here it is!"

"My God!" That was Malleson. "Let me see."

There was a long pause, broken only by what sounded like the rustling of paper. The silence was more disturbing than the noise had been, the tension in Justin's mind became almost unbearable; he was at the point of screaming again.

Then, still out of sight, Malleson said, "Yes, that's it. Come with me."

Eyes wide open now, Justin sat upright on the bed. The others appeared, Malleson in the lead. He was carrying a document in both hands, held out as if he wanted to read it. He drew close to Justin and demanded:

"How can you explain the presence of Mrs. Pantanelli's will behind your writing desk, Mr. Gray?"

The *will?* The missing will. It didn't make any sense at all. In a way this seemed the most incredible thing of all—the stolen will here, in *his* flat.

Justin said hoarsely, "I can't explain it. I didn't put it there."

"Didn't you?" asked Malleson heavily. "I see. Be advised by me, Mr. Gray, and get legal advice immediately."

He turned and went out. The other plainclothesman and the policeman followed, and went down the stairs. The front door closed with a snap of finality. Footsteps sounded on the gravel of the drive, and then he heard Malleson say:

"You'll stay here, Smith, and I want a note of everyone who calls."

"Yes, sir."

"Good night."

"Good night, sir."

A car door slammed and an engine started up.

Justin thought, legal advice. He could hardly think clearly, but he knew that was good advice. Legal advice, good advice, but who could advise him? Jacob Freeman? Young Joshua Freeman? Ross? No, they were all right for conveyancing, drawing up wills and agreements, but he needed good advice. He was under suspicion of murder of a woman whom he had liked and befriended half of his life.

Why didn't they believe him? To whom should he turn?

He thought vaguely of Tomlinson, the chairman of the museum committee. He had been a well-known barrister, hadn't he? Would he help? He might recommend someone even if he wouldn't do anything himself. Justin glanced at the clock by his bedside; it was twenty past three. You couldn't ring a comparative stranger, especially a semi-invalid, in the middle of the night. Why hadn't they turned the light off? It was shining straight into his eyes. He turned his head away from it, but knew that he would never get to sleep.

"Mr. Justin!"

A voice sounded from a long way off.

"*Mr. Justin!*"

It was a woman—it was Bertha Briggs!

"Mr. Justin, *please* wake up."

He opened his eyes, expecting to see the light on; instead, it was daylight, but the curtains were drawn to keep out the sun. Bertha, troubled eyes clouded, stood by the side of the bed with a tea tray in her hands.

Justin grunted.

"Oh, Mr. Justin, I thought you were never going to wake up!" She looked tremendously relieved. "It's half-past ten. When you didn't come in I thought I'd better come and wake you. There . . . there's such an awful rumor going around."

Justin struggled up. The pain in his head was still there, but not so acute. His mouth was parched, he could hardly wait for the tea. He was too bleary-eyed to see Bertha clearly, noting only that she was wearing the same flowered dress that she had worn yesterday.

"Pour me out a cup," he begged.

She put the tray at the foot of the bed, and poured.

"Such an *awful* rumor, Mr. Justin."

She handed him a steaming cup.

"Thank you. What is the rumor about?"

"Well, they *say* Mrs. Pantanelli's been murdered," announced Bertha.

"Yes, I knew that last night," Justin said, quite calmly. "Why did you come to see how I was, instead of one of my cousins, Bertha?"

"Well, Mr. Hugo isn't in, and Mr. Maurice had to go before the planning committee about the conversion of Holmsleigh into flats, and Mr. Alan had an appointment. I thought someone ought to come. So . . . so you *knew*?" She sounded as if she could not believe her ears.

"Yes, I knew. Will you telephone Mr. Tomlinson for me? Tell him it's an urgent personal matter. Then go back to the office and stay there until I arrive."

"I'll see to it," Bertha promised. She dialed a number without having to look it up; she had a photographic memory for numbers. "I've got the copies of . . . of poor Mrs. Pantanelli's dying statement, Mr. Justin."

"Put them on that table, will you?"

She did so, and then her whole expression changed, as if she thought that whoever was at the other end of the telephone could see her.

"Oh, Mr. Tomlinson, Mr. Justin Gray would be grateful for a word in confidence with you. . . . Please hold on."

"I'll come and see you at once," Tomlinson said. "Of course I will help if I can."

Tomlinson listened to Justin for nearly an hour, asked a number of questions that seemed to have no special significance, and then stood up from his chair in the living room and spoke quietly, impressively. As chairman of the museum committee he had always seemed too precise, too pedantic, something of an old woman. Now he was a different man, lucid and incisive.

"From what you've told me, the police are very sure of themselves. And from what I know of Malleson, he wouldn't have said so much to you unless he felt certain. Some of his behavior puzzles me, but he's too good a policeman not to have a satisfactory explanation. Why he allowed Dr. Nash to be present at his first interview for instance. And you don't appear to have many—if any—witnesses to testify for you. Malleson made it clear that this is your word against an impressive weight of evidence. And we must assume from what you tell me that he may charge you with the murder of Mrs. Pantanelli."

Justin felt quite sick. "There simply aren't any grounds for it," he said helplessly.

"So you say now. *Are* you sure, Justin? No, don't lose your temper—just ask yourself whether it is possible you have done some things without either—a—knowing of them at the time or—b—forgetting them afterward."

Justin gripped the arms of his chair. "In other words, am I mad?" he demanded hoarsely.

"In other words, are there two Justin Grays?" asked Tomlinson. "Now, *please* don't raise your voice, just believe I want to help in any way I can. . . . You are a most unusual man, you know, and you live under greater pressures than you realize. To adopt and adhere to a rigid code of behavior in today's society is a very great strain. There are simpler cases—where a man will on no account use bad language even though everyone about him does. Under an anaesthetic that same man will probably utter the most extreme obscenities. He is no longer exerting the iron self-control essential if he is to conform to his own high standards. I remember a case some fifteen years ago, when a man had two selves—one behaving in exactly the opposite way to the other. I had the help of an old friend then, and I think he would be very interested in this case, too. A Dr. Cellini, a consultant psychiatrist—but we mentioned him in committee only yesterday, didn't we?"

Justin said heavily, painfully, "Yes, we did. Why . . . I mean what purpose would it serve if I were to see him?"

"I think it would serve to establish whether you are telling all the truth, or whether your subconscious is concealing some of it," said Tomlinson. "I presume that *is* what you want, Justin? To find out the truth?"

Chapter 13

DR. CELLINI

"What you are anxious to know," said Dr. Emmanuel Cellini, "is whether you have been lying to yourself or whether—"

"Dr. Cellini," Justin interrupted icily, "I am tired of discussing this matter with consultants who assume that I am either mad or a consummate hypocrite."

The small, elderly man in whose living room he sat looked at him steadily for a long time, and then began to smile. Justin had been surprised, at first, when he had met Emmanuel Cellini, for he seemed a gentle, benevolent, unforceful old man, with beautiful silvery hair and a big mustache of the same hue tinged very slightly with a color that—in the sunlight now streaming through the window—looked like gold. He spoke in a quiet voice with an attractive accent, his command of English perfect enough, though at times a little pedantic.

"Yes," he said. "I understand you perfectly. Goodness is the last quality people expect to find in human beings. When they come upon it they are immediately suspicious. Goodness is always too good to be true in the eyes of the world."

With these words Cellini seemed to Justin to grow in stature. His voice remained soft, his expression a little sad, but not despairing, not distressed. In a showcase by his side were the three Cellini gold caskets, and it was the sun, reflecting on these, that cast the golden tinge onto this man. His face was small, with regular features, his skin without blemish.

The last word fell into silence, and he waited.

"I will answer any question you put to me," Justin said, feeling suddenly very humble, almost ashamed.

"I'm glad you have decided so wisely. Mr. Tomlinson will sit with us, and afterward he may ask other questions that will help him to confound the police."

Justin had almost forgotten that the barrister was present; Tomlinson sat in one corner in a winged armchair, his legs stretched out, the ankles crossed. He raised a hand in acknowledgment of Cellini's adjuration.

It was nearly six o'clock, and Justin had been here for an hour, talking only about what had happened, obsessed by the plight in which he found himself.

"So I repeat," went on Cellini, "you are anxious to know whether you have been lying to yourself or whether your peculiar rigidity of principle has goaded others to try falsely to prove you are a liar."

Warmth began to steal through the chill in Justin's veins. "Yes," he said, "that's exactly what I want to know."

"If I have understood the background of the case properly, you have often opposed your three partners in business policy."

"Yes. Frequently."

"Over how long a period?" asked Cellini.

"Five years at least."

"Will you enlarge on that? Be a little more specific?"

"When I first inherited my share in the business from my father, I didn't know much about the business itself. I'd been in Africa, half thinking of farming there. Only Maurice and Hugo were active partners at that time, and I accepted their decisions until I realized what they were doing. When Alan came into it, he saw things their way rather than mine."

"Is there a formal partnership?" asked Cellini.

"No. There never was, even in the early days, and there isn't now. Then it was shared three ways, now it's shared four ways—each of us takes the same amount out of the business and has an equal say. I'm often outvoted, but if I really dig myself in they have to give way. And one of us becomes chairman of meetings each year—this year it's my turn. Any two of us can sign checks, and . . . well, it all works fairly well. As I say I didn't know much, and in the early days went along with what they were doing."

"What *were* they doing?" asked Cellini.

"Buying property at very low prices and selling it at high prices," said Justin.

"Do you *really* believe that is a crime?" asked Cellini.

Justin hesitated a long time before answering. "I think it is wrong if you have advance information about the value of a property that makes it more valuable than its owner realizes. Such as foreknowledge of a town-planning scheme, or road widening—that kind of thing. It can be a criminal offense to get advance information, too—I'm not absolutely sure that my partners don't bribe town-planning staff to let something out."

"It could indeed be criminal," said Cellini, and he glanced at Tomlinson. "Couldn't it, James?"

Tomlinson took his pipe from his mouth and said cryptically, "Yes."

Cellini turned back to Justin. "Did your partners do this kind of thing often?"

"They often tried to."

"What first aroused your conscience, Mr. Gray?"

Had anyone else posed the question in that way, Justin would have suspected sarcasm; from Cellini he accepted it as a literal inquiry.

I found they had formed certain companies, then acted for these companies. One company bought a cottage in a row of terraced houses owned by an elderly couple who had to move into a flat. The woman was crippled with arthritis. The cottage was bought for seven hundred and fifty pounds and sold for over two thousand a few months later. Had the couple received twice the sum they were paid, they would have been in comfortable circumstances. As it was, they had a hard struggle to make ends meet. In point of fact," he went on, "they had to separate and live in institutions, but that happened some time afterward. My quarrel with the partners came when I realized that they had full knowledge of town-planning schemes that would put up the value of the cottage. I told them I thought it was sharp practice and would never go along with it."

"I see. And their reaction?"

Slowly, Justin answered, "We haven't really got on well since. Nearly every meeting is a dog fight. They once talked of buying me out, but they hadn't the money to make an offer— and I don't think I would have accepted. It would simply have given them a clear hand to do what they wanted."

"I see. So as things are, they see an opportunity for such a transaction, and you prevent it."

Justin hesitated.

"Or *don't* you?" asked Cellini mildly. "Do circumstances alter cases—I believe that is the phrase. Are there exceptions to your rule, Mr. Gray?"

"No exceptions if I am certain the rule has to be applied," answered Justin.

"Who decides whether it should be or not?"

"I do."

"Doesn't that put you in a very arbitrary position?" inquired Cellini.

"It sometimes puts me in a difficult one," retorted Justin.

"Surely a thing is right or it is not right?"

"There are cases—a lot of cases—where the excess profit might not materialize. If there is a reasonable risk of this, and if I stopped a sale by telling the owner he ought to get much more, then he might later have to sell at an even lower figure. That would hardly be right, either."

"I see," said Cellini. "A very fine distinction."

"Good point," Tomlinson remarked unexpectedly.

"Shall we discuss that more fully later?" Cellini's voice held a note of mild remonstrance.

"Sorry." Tomlinson subsided gracefully.

"Thank you. Now, is this the *only* kind of difference you have with your partners?" Cellini asked Justin.

Justin found himself laughing. "It certainly isn't!"

"What others are there?"

"Such issues as overgenerous recommendations for mortgage . . . acceptance of bribes called commission to give one buyer an advantage over another, without benefiting the owner . . . overlenient or oversevere valuations to give an owner an unjust advantage—"

Cellini interrupted. "Are large sums involved in these transactions?"

"No, not large—usually a few hundred pounds at most, except in certain property purchases."

"Such as the instance you stated earlier, the instance of the attempt to buy Mrs. Pantanelli's property, which appears to have sparked off this present trouble," suggested Cellini.

"That's the largest deal ever attempted," said Justin.

"And your cousins would have proceeded without hesitation but for you."

"I am sure they would."

"Were you tempted—in view of the fact that the old lady was so advanced in age, and could not possibly benefit?"

Justin shifted in his chair. The sun had moved and no longer shone on the gold caskets, and Cellini's hair and mustache had become a soft, silvery white. In the subdued light, he looked younger, too, rather like an aged cherub.

"Not really tempted," Justin said at last. "I considered it, trying to see their point of view." He suddenly remembered Charlotte saying that if he bent over backward he would get a distorted impression. The recollection hurt: Why *had* she turned on him in such a way? "There could be no question that it was wrong."

"You are absolutely convinced of that?" insisted Cellini.

"Yes," said Justin flatly. "I have no doubt at all."

"Could there be any other reason why you should wish to prevent this sale?"

"No. None at all. What are you suggesting?"

"Do you *like* your cousins, Mr. Gray?"

"Not . . . not particularly."

"Do you approve of them?"

"Not very much."

"Would you prefer them to be in an unsuccessful business?"

Justin looked astonished. "Good lord, no! Why on earth should I?"

"You might reason that if they remained too long in a business that made little profit they might take positions elsewhere and leave you in sole control, taking only their share of the profits. Wouldn't you like that, Mr. Gray?"

Justin felt the familiar tension returning, found himself gripping the arms of his chair tightly; and the tautness at the back of his head and his forehead became noticeable for the first time in hours.

Harshly, he said, "Yes, I would."

"Ah. Have you ever said so?"

"I've often said that the partners take too much out—the profits aren't large enough to pay the four of us a good salary."

"And what is their answer?"

"That we should expand the business," answered Justin.

"By transactions of a kind of which you do not approve?"

"Yes," Justin said unevenly. "Yes, they want me out. They would gladly buy me out now. They would get the money somehow."

"And you want *them* out!"

"Unless they work better, yes, I do."

"Do you work any harder than they?" asked Cellini.

"I think so."

"*Do you?*" Cellini almost barked.

"Twice, three times as hard—*yes!*"

Even as he shouted the answer Justin recalled his own misgivings of the previous day, how he had equated his time off for his committees with theirs for their particular hobbies and interests. He was sweating. His head was splitting, and he felt almost as bad as he had the previous night. He expected Cellini to go on with his questions, perhaps to challenge that last answer, but the older man sat very still, his pale hands on the arms of his chair. The last of the sunlight had gone from the room, and the kindly face was touched with shadow.

Justin sprang up. "Yes," he said savagely, "I do. I take as much time off as they do, it makes no difference to the firm whether I take it off for local committees or they take it off for golf or bridge or girl friends. But while I'm working I work much more solidly, more thoroughly. The one who really works her fingers to the bone is Miss Briggs, our senior clerk. *She* may have cause for complaint, but the others haven't the slightest."

Cellini said, "Sit down, Mr. Gray. I am sorry to distress you. I am trying, you see, to find out what you think, as distinct from what you want us—and others—to think you think. It is very evident that you have weighed this situation most carefully. You are not assuming superiority because you spend your time away from the office on good works."

"I'd like to raise a point," Tomlinson put in, pipe pointing toward them.

"I . . . oh, very well, James."

"Justin is wrong. It does make a difference that he serves on all these committees and does a great deal of work for the community. He may not know it and may not plan it, but it is this that influences a great number of the firm's clients."

"That is indeed a point of material interest," said Cellini approvingly. "I should never really try to stop you, James. However, you confront Mr. Gray with yet another dilemma. If as a result of his doing good, he creates good will for his company, is he as single-minded in his doing good as he would like to think? Or is he, subconsciously, taking on these charitable works in order to improve his income?"

Cellini was smiling at Justin as he finished.

"*Was* that how you reasoned?" demanded Tomlinson.

"It . . . well, yes," Justin admitted. "I hadn't got so far but—"

"Good God, man, you're trying to be a plaster saint!" exclaimed Tomlinson.

"You put a very heavy burden on yourself," Cellini said, "and you examine your own motives too closely—using, if I may say so, a mental microscope through which to study and to enlarge moral issues. How long have you thought like this, Justin?"

It was the first time that Cellini had used his Christian name, and it was almost as if he did so in order to soften the impact of his words. Although very much more gently, they said what Charlotte had said at the cottage last night.

"Did you hear me?" Cellini insisted.

"I've . . . I've forgotten what you said," Justin muttered.

"I asked you how long you had been putting your motives under the microscope in this way," repeated Cellini. "It is—it can only be—very wearing on the nerves. You live alone, I understand."

"Yes."

"Do you share these critical self-analyses with anyone else?"

"I . . . no. No, not now."

"So you used to."

"Yes. Mrs. Pantanelli used to be interested."

"*Really!*" ejaculated Cellini.

"Were you such good friends as all that?" demanded Tomlinson, as if astounded.

"We . . . we saw a lot of things in the same way," answered Justin huskily. "As a matter of fact, it was really through her that I began to check what I was doing. I'd always been . . . dull, I suppose. Pi, they called it at school. I never saw any advantage in lying, or cribbing, or using bad language, but it wasn't until after I got to know Mrs. Pantanelli that I really thought deeply about it. She—" He broke off, and after a pause, began again. "My father and his brother-in-law started the business, thirty years ago. Soon after I joined the firm I learned that my father had . . . had used the very methods I don't like. During his day at least two families were ruined. One man committed suicide because he was heavily in debt. If he had received the true value of his house it would have saved him. I'd never liked the harsh side of business. That's really why I contemplated living abroad. Then my father died, about seven years ago. I came back to clear things up, and . . . well, I committed myself to running that business in a way no one could fault. It seemed to me the least I could do to make amends for the way it had been run before." Justin began to move about the room, staring at the caskets with no more interest than if they had been pieces of pottery. "My father's will left a twenty-five percent share to me provided I took an active part in the business. If I didn't, then my share would be divided among the other partners. My choice was either to hand my shares over and let them run the business their way or go in and try to make the others run it as I thought they should."

He moved to the window. Outside there were trees and open ground, families playing, people walking, dogs frisking, two boys flying kites with great concentration. They might have belonged to another world.

Without looking around, he went on, "I couldn't make up my mind. I wanted to get away from Hodenham, from England, I abhorred the way things were going here. And I knew what a struggle it would be with Maurice, relentless, hurtful, never-ending. How right I was!" he interpolated bitterly. "On the other hand, if I were to abdicate, I was really letting down people whom the others might injure—I was washing my hands of the whole affair."

He stopped, a catch in his breath. He spun around.

"Have *you* ever felt like Pontius Pilate?" he demanded hoarsely. "Have you?"

Chapter 14

THE ESSENCE OF
THE PROBLEM

DR. CELLINI STOOD for the first time and drew nearer to Justin, whose face was almost distorted with passion, whose eyes reflected the strange, consuming self-torture he was inflicting upon himself.

"It isn't necessary to have felt as you do in order to understand how you feel," Cellini declared. "I know exactly what you mean. This struggle is not unique, Justin. Some would call it—forgive me—overzealous, even a form of religious mania."

"But I'm not religious!"

"You are confused by a label," said Cellini. "You may not conform to any dogma, but religions—what *is* the pursuit of goodness but a religion? Can you answer that?"

Justin closed his eyes, and after a long time said, "I see what you mean."

"I hoped you would. What made you decide to go into business, after all?"

"I discussed it with Mrs. Pantanelli."

"Ah!"

"And she felt as I did, that the only way I could live with myself was to go into the business. It meant giving up all thought of emigrating, but when I came face to face with the choice, I knew it was already decided."

"But you hated what you had to do?"

"I disliked . . . oh yes! I hated it."

"Has it been as bad as you anticipated?"

"There was the compensation I hadn't expected," Justin replied slowly. "I enjoy the committee work, the sense of being part of the community, and I'm not sorry I stayed in England. Even the business itself hasn't always been so bad. Some aspects of it I like. One meets a lot of people, one can—even if it does sound smug!—do a little good. It's a funny thing," he added, "but you can, literally, enjoy another's happiness. When a young couple who are getting married find just what they want—" He broke off, but neither of the older men spoke, until he went on roughly, "The only real trouble has been the conflict with Maurice. It wasn't always in the open, but it was liable to flare up at any time."

"And do the others invariably agree with him?"

"He always talks them around, even if they're against a project at first."

"Justin," said Cellini, moving back to his seat, "have you never been able to share this feeling, this sensitivity, with anyone else?"

"Two people," Justin answered promptly. "Mrs. Pantanelli, but she began to wander in her mind long before she had the first stroke. And"—his voice dropped to a whisper—"Moira."

"Moira," echoed Cellini gently.

"I was in love with her, and I could talk to her. She felt much the same as I did." He caught his breath. "She was killed in a road accident."

Into the silence that followed, Tomlinson murmured, "I remember, Justin. A tragic affair."

Justin didn't speak.

"And has there been no one else?" asked Cellini, still gently.

"Not really. Not really," repeated Justin. He went back to his chair and dropped heavily into it. "I'd never met anyone I thought could understand until the night before last. Mrs.

Warwick, I mean. And it was soon evident that, even if she understood, she rejected the whole idea—she could think of nothing but compromise. Compromise!" he echoed bitterly. "I think that's worse than living by unethical standards. To know what you should do and not do it—that *is* hypocrisy."

"And your cousin Maurice threatened to prove you were a hypocrite?"

"Yes."

"Had he ever said such a thing before?"

"He'd never let himself go so far before."

"Do you know why he was particularly antagonistic on this occasion?"

"A big sum of money was at stake."

"That may indeed be the reason," Cellini conceded, speaking more to himself than Justin. "We must find out. Immediately after this confrontation, you say, the trouble began—the unpleasant incidents, I mean."

"The same evening, yes," answered Justin.

"Have you considered the possibility that these unpleasant acts were committed by someone other than Maurice?"

"I hadn't, until Inspector Malleson suggested it."

"I see," said Cellini, and he walked to a cabinet of beautifully inlaid ivory, opened it, and took out a decanter of sherry and three glasses, then a silver jar of exquisite workmanship. He put these on a small table and began to unstopper the decanter. "And now you are in danger of being charged with murdering the one woman who truly befriended and helped you." He poured, and the gurgle of the sherry was the only sound until each of them had a glass in his hand. "Did you kill her, Justin?"

Justin almost dropped the glass. "What a question to ask!"

"Will you answer it, please?" Cellini was standing over him, very close.

"I did not kill her!"

"Thank you," said Cellini.

"Three people, all reputable and presumably reliable witnesses, say they saw you at Hilltop yesterday afternoon," Tomlinson murmured.

Justin, hardly understanding the significance of this remark, answered flatly, "I was not there."

"So you say three people lied." Tomlinson frowned and sat upright in his chair, as if the sherry had activated him. "Is that what you mean?"

"Or three people were mistaken," suggested Cellini mildly.

"*Three* people mistaken?" Tomlinson sounded incredulous. "You might cast doubt on one, but three—it's not reasonable. The fact that you were there doesn't necessarily mean that you poisoned Mrs. Pantanelli, but if you deny it you will have convicted yourself of lying. We've a difficult enough task without having to clear that hurdle."

Justin looked at him, startled, but found himself turning back to Cellini as he said, "*I did not go to Hilltop yesterday afternoon.*"

"Unless," murmured Cellini, "you went without realizing it."

"That's impossible!"

"I assure you such things *do* happen."

"I don't mean it's beyond the realm of possibility," Justin said. "I mean I can account for every minute of my time yesterday afternoon—and *you* can account for it from five o'clock onward."

"The crucial time was between three o'clock and four," Tomlinson pointed out.

"I was in my office."

"You were seen to go to your office, you then went down to your cousin Maurice's office and discovered he was out. You called a meeting for three-thirty to inform your cousins you had consulted the police. It took place earlier. You went into your office and, ostensibly, stayed until nearly five o'clock.

You were five minutes late at the museum," Tomlinson reminded him, in a dry voice, "and during the whole of it you
were very preoccupied."

"Well?" Justin barked.

"You *could* have left by the back door of the building—a
door, incidentally, which you refuse to have locked although
Miss Briggs has often requested you to do so—without being
seen. Your car is parked three minutes from the back door.
You could have driven to Mrs. Pantanelli's, seen her, administered the poison, and returned—all within twenty-five minutes. I know you could," Tomlinson digressed dryly. "I did
it—including going into the house and staying there for nearly
ten minutes. Can you prove that you didn't do these things?"

Slowly, helplessly, Justin said, "I know that I didn't. I can't
prove it."

"The jury will be given proof, in evidence, that you did go
out," Tomlinson told him.

"But it's not true!" cried Justin. "And what are you trying
to do—tell me I'm a congenital liar or that I *am* mad? I can
remember sitting at my desk, going over everything that had
happened, baffled by the whole affair. I didn't leave the
office until just before five. I had to hurry to get across to the
museum as soon as I did. For God's sake, *believe* me!"

There was passion in his voice, passion and hopelessness.

"Justin, *I* believe you," Cellini said. "James will not believe
anything that cannot be proved."

"In this case, it *has* to be proved," declared Tomlinson.

"Who is supposed to have seen me?" demanded Justin,
more quietly. "Tell me that."

"That we don't know. But I spent some time with the
police this morning, as your legal representative. I hope you
approve," Tomlinson added.

"I'd approve much more if you would believe me," Justin
muttered.

"I cannot prove to the jury anything that you cannot prove

to me," argued Tomlinson. "Malleson was helpful. He told me that he has these witnesses—two who saw you leave your office building, three who saw you at Hilltop. He also let me see the pathologist's report—the autopsy was held this morning. Digitalin was injected into Mrs. Pantanelli's right arm, between the elbow and shoulder. She was not, as it happened, being treated with digitalin—she *had* been for nearly two years before, but her reaction to the drug had been unsatisfactory, and it had been discontinued for some weeks. Whoever administered the injection must have known—I should say *probably* knew—about the original treatment, but not that it had been discontinued in the recent past."

"In my considerable experience with police officials, the attitude and behavior of Inspector Malleson is unusual," Cellini remarked. "At times he appears to be hostile, at others, excessively well-disposed."

"He wants the truth," said Tomlinson. "He also feels that Justin has attempted to fool him. He's been overworking, and between you and me, he's having domestic trouble. His wife resents the hours he puts in on his job. That's almost a policeman's occupational hazard," Tomlinson added, "but it needs an exceptional woman to cope with it."

"Do you know why he allowed Dr. Nash to be present when he first interviewed Justin?" asked Cellini.

"I know the reason he gives, and it can hardly be challenged. Justin obviously wasn't well. Nash was there to make sure the police did not take advantage of his condition. You were in a state of shock," Tomlinson added to Justin. "Did you realize it?"

"Yes, I suppose so," Justin said. "My head was splitting, all I wanted was to rest." He noticed the two men frown at each other meaningfully, and his voice sharpened. "Are you still harping on the possibility that I'm suffering from schizophrenia?"

"I do not think you are, but we must have expert opinion," said Cellini. "I would like you to be examined by another consultant, though—not because I think you are ill, *please* try not to get so excited!—but if this case ever gets to court we shall need all the expert evidence we can get. And whatever else, you *are* overharried to a point of exhaustion. If you weren't, you wouldn't be so very much on edge."

"Or is that normal for you?" Tomlinson put in.

Slowly, Justin admitted, "I *do* get more edgy lately."

"You have been living on your nerves—demanding far too much of yourself," Cellini almost scolded. Then he added, briskly for him, "Let us consider certain facts and their implications. The dogs *were* put at your doors. The bird *was* left on your desk. The bees *were* lured to the cottage. The timing, in each case, was obviously intended to distress you acutely. The boy Micky Jones did do these things—his confession has been corroborated by some of his friends, and he was seen by neighbors leaving the garden of the house where you live, and also coming out of the alley by your offices about the time the bird was placed on your desk. And he says that you paid him to."

"But I didn't—" began Justin wildly.

"Wait, please! The offices of Freeman and Ross *were* burgled. As far as the lawyers can tell, the only thing stolen was Mrs. Pantanelli's will. The will *was* found behind a writing desk in your flat. These facts are all indisputable. The police will need to find a very convincing motive if they are to satisfy a jury that you did these things yourself."

"I—did—not—do—them. I—did—not—pay—James—or— anyone—else—to—do—them. I—do—not—know—how— the—will—got—into—my—flat. *Are you going to believe me or aren't you?*"

Justin realized that he was shouting. One half of his mind hated what he was doing, even fought against it, but the other half made him raise his voice, made him lose his temper, go almost berserk. As he shouted, the tautness at his head became unbearable.

He did not know that his eyes were glassy and staring, that his lips quivered, that his whole body shook. He did not even notice when he knocked the sherry glass off the arm of his chair.

"I believe you," Cellini told him gently.

"You're only saying that! Every question you ask shows you don't!"

"I believe you," Cellini repeated.

"I don't believe you," Tomlinson stated flatly.

"The hell you don't!" cried Justin. "At least that's honest, but why the devil—"

"And bellowing like a beaten bully won't help you," Tomlinson said coldly. "If you'd lie once, you'd lie a dozen times."

"*I haven't lied at all!*"

"Yes you have."

"James—"

"But he *has* lied. He may have had a good reason for it but he has lied."

"*I—have—not—lied!*" Justin almost spat.

"You lied about not knowing the contents of Mrs. Pantanelli's will. You spread the story that you believed most of her money was going to charities so that your interest in her could never seem suspect."

"I don't know the contents—I never knew them—I neither know nor care whether charities get the money or not. She once told me that's what she would do."

"You knew the contents. You stole the will to check that there were no codicils. Your foreknowledge made you adamant over allowing your company to make a profit that you would have to share with them."

"This is crazy," Justin gasped. "Absolutely crazy!"

"It is cold common sense," declared Tomlinson. "You had

reason to believe *you* were the main beneficiary, that when she died you would inherit most of her property. This is why you could be so high and mighty about the houses your partners wanted to buy. You pretended to be utterly disinterested in your friendship for Mrs. Pantanelli, but you certainly were not. How are you going to convince me, or a jury, that you didn't kill your close and long-standing friend in order to inherit? Under Mrs. Pantanelli's will you inherit over a hundred thousand pounds. *That's* worth breaking a lifelong charade of integrity for, isn't it?"

When Justin didn't reply, just sat there shocked and incredulous, Tomlinson went on in a stern, accusing voice:

"You have betrayed your own standards. You have killed in cold blood. I do not think you are worth defending."

Chapter 15

THE COLLAPSE

JUSTIN TRIED to get out of his chair.

His legs refused to obey him; there was no strength in his arms; and he could not hoist himself. He wanted to throw himself at Tomlinson, who stood in accusing silence, like a statue to retribution. He did not move. Cellini seemed to have disappeared. Justin's lips worked. The tension and pain at the back of his head and his forehead was unbearable—absolutely unbearable. It was as if someone had put a steel helmet over his skull and was pressing it tighter and tighter.

With his conscious mind he thought, *Everyone, everyone is accusing me. No one believes me, but I've told the truth, the truth, the truth.* This room, like the landing of his own flat yesterday, seemed to be going around and around; so did Tomlinson. Tomlinson, the precise, the pedantic, now the accuser. Tomlinson, to whom he had gone for help.

Why were they doing this? Why didn't his head stop aching?

It was agony. The steel cowl was pressing on an artery now; his head throbbed to the beat of his heart. *Thump, thump, thump, thump.* He couldn't stand it any more. *Thump, thump, thump, thump.*

Someone was loosening his collar and tie. Someone was putting brandy to his lips, lifting him, stretching him out on a couch, which had cushions as soft as clouds.

He was aware, as if it were happening somewhere else and in another time, of a blood pressure pump, the bag about his arm; of the cold of a stethoscope on his chest and back, of prodding, probing fingers, of hands or fingers at his head, of a light in his eyes, of quiet voices.

Soon he was aware that he was no longer being examined. Someone was putting a cover over him, a cool sheet. It was a man he had never seen before. Dr. Cellini was in the room, so was Tomlinson. The furious hate he had felt for Tomlinson had faded now; he felt no emotion at all. No hate, no anger, no resentfulness. He existed, but he did not think or feel.

"Well?" That was Tomlinson.

"I'd need a cardiac check, urine test, and blood test before I could be sure," the stranger said, "but I would expect them to confirm what I think now."

"And what *is* your diagnosis?" inquired Cellini.

The strange thing was that, although this concerned him, Justin did not care what the answer was. The cushions were soft, he was very comfortable, there was not even pressure at his head.

"Nervous prostration," the doctor answered. "He needs a long rest."

"No more than that?"

"I can find nothing to indicate it," the stranger answered. "When can I have those specimens?"

"Very soon, I've no doubt. When can you take the cardiogram?"

"Tomorrow morning."

"Will he be well enough to go to the hospital?"

"Oh yes. A few hours rest and he'll recharge his batteries, at least for a few hours. That's what he's been doing—using up all his reserves of nervous energy, driving himself beyond his limit. Did he crack suddenly?"

"Apparently, yes."

"I don't mean today. . . ."

"No. This was to some degree induced." Tomlinson was speaking. "According to several people who know him well, he seemed normal until the day before yesterday. Rather more short-tempered than usual, perhaps, but no more than that. Then he ran into one shock after another, and presumably that caused the collapse."

"He'll be all right when he's rested," the unknown doctor insisted.

They were both talking as if Justin couldn't hear, but not only was he hearing, he was beginning to *feel*. This mattered; this was good news. He was better already.

They all went out of the room, leaving him alone. It was so pleasant and quiet and comfortable, and he could think reflectively. There was another, reassuring element: his outbursts of temper had a reason—not an excuse, a physical reason. Temper. How he had flown at Tomlinson! It wasn't surprising, even now he could think that—after all, the man had accused him of being a liar, a cheat, and a murderer. Well, he wasn't. "Sticks and stones can break my bones but words can never hurt me." Nonsense. Words could hurt like the very devil. Not Tomlinson now, but some words. *His* words. Charlotte's words.

For the first time since he had come around, he felt a twinge of hurt. Why *had* she talked as she had? Why hadn't he been more patient? At least he hadn't gone for her as he had for Tomlinson, but he could recall her expression, the distress on her face, before she had left him. Strange that she should have come into his life without the slightest warning, and walked out of it just as abruptly. Fate. Fate? Was it fate that, having met a woman for whom he could feel so quickly, he had to resent everything she said? Now he could persuade himself that she had meant only to help him.

Like Tomlinson? Or was he fooling himself about them both?

The door opened, and Dr. Cellini came in, alone.

For the first time, Justin realized that it had grown dark.

Cellini closed the door and switched on a nearby light, then drew close to Justin. He must have noticed that Justin's eyes were open, for he said:

"How are you, Justin?"

"Much . . . much calmer, thanks."

"I hoped you would be." Cellini hitched up a chair and sat down, placing his pale hands on the chair arms. "How much do you recall of what happened?" he asked in a quiet, relaxed way.

"You mean the doctor's examination?"

"Ah. So you were fully aware of what was going on."

"I think so," Justin said, and added with dry humor, "Even though Tomlinson probably won't agree."

"If you can tell him what happened, he will agree," Cellini assured him. "I don't think we should talk any more just now. We can deal with the situation better tomorrow, when you're rested. I would like you to stay here for the night. We have a comfortable spare room and it will be no trouble. You have been alone with your thoughts far too much, Justin, so please don't protest. Relax here, and be sure you will be very welcome."

So he didn't have to get up, go out, walk through his garden half-fearful of what he would find, go upstairs and begin to get his evening meal ready, put on the record player, or, if there was anything worth seeing, switch on television. He had nothing to do but relax.

"I'm very grateful," he said. "I can't tell you how grateful I am."

About the time that Justin was relaxing in the luxurious realization that he had no effort to make, Eric Malleson was sitting in his office studying the reports in front of him. There was the autopsy report; there was a photostat copy of Mrs. Pantanelli's will; there were witnesses' statements, all corroborated by at least one independent witness, and yet there were still two questions in his mind.

First: why had Justin Gray behaved as he had? Could it be—as Dr. Nash had suggested—he was not quite right in the head?

Second: should he, Malleson recommend to the divisional superintendent that Justin Gray be charged with murder?

And yet a third question, a personal one: what attitude should he adopt with his wife when he reached home.

More and more these days he worked late, not only because it postponed the inevitable clash, but because sometimes she was in bed, asleep or so nearly asleep that she was unlikely to quarrel.

He checked and rechecked the witnesses' statements. Some were obviously open to doubt, such as young Micky Jones', but the corroboration from neighbors could not be challenged. There had been five different people who would all swear to seeing Justin Gray at times when Gray had denied being in the vicinity.

That made Gray out a liar.

At certain times Malleson found this almost impossible to believe; at others he felt so sure of it that he almost hated Justin for his hypocrisy.

Why on earth should he have behaved in such a way?

That was the obvious question and the one the divisional superintendent would want answered. Why should Justin play such pranks on himself? Either he was a bit touched or else he wanted to create a wave of sympathy for himself in a deliberate attempt to appear as the victim of a campaign. This could only be because he wanted to prove someone else guilty—and he could not have made it clearer that Maurice Mendelson was to be the man.

These things would have been puzzling enough in themselves, but the theft of the will made it more peculiar. Why should Justin steal a will when he almost certainly knew the contents? And, having stolen it, why should he hide it in his own flat, where it was bound to be incriminating?

"It doesn't make sense," Malleson muttered to himself in exasperation.

He had spent much of the day questioning the staff at Mendelson and Gray's—and questioning the other three partners. Each of them had denied any complicity; all of them had said that Justin had been acting strangely of late, had been edgy and short-tempered, so unlike him. The staff had also noticed these things. Even Bertha Briggs, loyal though she always was, had admitted she had noticed that Mr. Justin hadn't really been himself lately.

"I'll leave the whole thing until tomorrow," Malleson decided.

When he got home to his small new house on the Hill estate, his wife was asleep. He got his own supper, looked through the papers, turned on television for ten minutes, heard an epilogue without taking it in, and went to bed.

It didn't make sense, he kept repeating to himself.

Even Justin's lying made no sense. How could he hope to establish that he had been in one place when so many people had seen him in another? And why had he chosen this juncture to poison old Mrs. Pantanelli, unless he was desperately in need of money? There wasn't the slightest indication that he was in debt, but he might be. The possibility must be checked.

There was one other mystery Malleson wanted to solve: the part the woman known as Charlotte Warwick had played in this affair. Had she come into it solely by chance, as Justin Gray had said? And if that had been so, who had she been to visit in Hodenham?

"That's something I can find out," Malleson muttered. "I can start inquiries about it tomorrow."

The first thing he did, when he reached the office next morning, was to telephone his divisional superintendent, a man nearing retiring age, who knew every trick and every regulation in the police manual.

He listened. Then he said, "Find out where that woman stayed. . . . Check the hotel where Gray says he took her first. . . . Find out if Gray had any access to digitalin. . . . Watch Gray like a lynx. Where is he now?"

"Staying with Dr. Cellini," Malleson answered.

"That old busybody! When he comes back, have him watched night and day—in fact I'll arrange for someone to watch him at Cellini's. We want to keep Gray on edge. Check with me if there are any new developments, and in any case every afternoon before five o'clock and every morning before ten. All clear?"

"Yes, sir."

"If Gray shows any indication of leaving the district, pull him in."

"On what charge, sir?"

"Possession of stolen property—the old woman's will is enough for that," said the superintendent. "One other thing. Watch out for Cellini and Tomlinson. Cellini is as wily as a fox, believe me, and Tomlinson will prove black is white if you give him a chance. Don't hide anything from him, though. If he knows we're playing ball, he'll play ball with us."

"I'll keep him posted," Malleson promised, glad that he had been doing so all along.

"We want to make sure we know all the story before charging Gray," the superintendent finished. "One false move and Tomlinson and Cellini between them will make mincemeat out of us."

"On the face of it, what's your opinion, sir?" asked Malleson.

"It's just possible Gray is lying to protect someone else," his chief answered. "More likely, he's lying to protect himself." He sniffed audibly into the telephone. "Who else could have any motive for murdering Mrs. Pantanelli?"

"No one at all. Charities apart, he's the only beneficiary with more than a few hundred pounds to come," answered Malleson.

"Then you'll get him," the superintendent said. "It's only a matter of time."

Justin stayed at Dr. Cellini's for two nights, and on the second morning felt more invigorated and clear-minded than he had for months. On the previous morning he had been to the hospital in Wimbledon, and since then had seen the doctor's report: his heart was in excellent condition, he was simply suffering from overstrain. In his relief he had talked frankly to Cellini, finding him sympathetic and understanding, and Felisa Cellini, the psychiatrist's wife, kind and charming.

"You understand, you will get in touch with me and with James Tomlinson if there is any more to worry you," said Cellini. "You will *not* overwork. And you will watch and listen to your partners very carefully."

"I'll be good," promised Justin.

They both laughed.

As he drove to his apartment, first, to check that all was well, he had no apprehension; and none when he went upstairs. The daily maid had been in, and the place was in its usual meticulous order; milk, bread, everything he wanted was in the pantry or the refrigerator. He saw a police car outside and knew that he was being watched, but that did not worry him. It was after eleven o'clock when he reached the office, seeing the alertness on the expressions of the girls, the eagerness on Bertha's.

"Oh, Mr. Gray, I *am* glad to see you back." She stood away from him as if to judge more clearly. "And you look so much better, you really do."

"I feel fine," said Justin. "Where is everybody?"

"Mr. Alan's away with a cold," answered Bertha. "Mr. Hugo's gone over to the Ministry inquiry about the planning for the new shopping center, and Mr. Maurice is over at Abbey National. Some query cropped up about the mortgage for the Rennisons' place."

"And how have you all been getting on without me?" asked Justin dryly.

"Oh, we've missed you!"

"But everything's under control, thanks to Bertha Briggs."

"It's nice of you to say so," said Bertha. "I—oh, that's my call to Freeman and Ross. There's a query about a conveyance. Would you like some coffee?"

"You bring it up," Justin said.

His office door was open. On his desk was the mail for three days. He looked through it. There was nothing very special, either good or bad. There was also a scrawled note from Hugo:

"I'll be glad to see you when you're back."

Everything was normal, then—or it seemed to be. Was this because he was feeling so much better? Had he seen too many things distorted, because of what he now knew was a form of illness? Nervous exhaustion! He would have scoffed at such a phrase before.

He heard Bertha coming up the stairs, and saw her, coffee in hand.

"Here's your coffee, Mr. Justin. I think it's just as you like it." She placed an overfull mug in front of him. "I can't tell you how glad I am you've taken it so well, Mr. Justin—I hated to have to do it."

Idly, he asked, "Do what?"

"Oh, you know. I hated telling the police about you, but I knew you hadn't been well, you see. You were forgetting so many things. Anyhow, everything's all right now, thank goodness."

"Everything's fine," Justin said, but his heart began to contract. "Exactly what did you tell the police, Bertha?"

"Oh, you know," she repeated. "About seeing you talking to that Jones boy, and going out the afternoon before Mrs. Pantanelli died. I knew you would rather me tell the truth, but it's ever such a relief to know you don't mind. I—Mr. Justin! Mr. Justin! Are you all right?"

He put the mug down so heavily that hot coffee splashed over his hand. She looked horrified, quite unable to understand why he was so affected.

She couldn't possibly have seen him do either of these things. But Bertha Briggs would never lie.

Chapter 16

THE WOMAN WHO DISAPPEARED

"It's ALL RIGHT, Bertha," Justin said huskily. "Don't worry." He dabbed perfunctorily at the coffee on his hand and sleeve. "I just remembered something I'd forgotten, it's nothing to do with this."

That was a lie.

But he couldn't argue with her, he couldn't begin all over again, especially with Bertha. He couldn't start to make her understand how terrifying it was to be told she had seen him in a place and at a time he could not remember.

She went out, obviously uneasy.

He wiped his forehead with the back of his hand, and then drank what was left of the coffee. Finished, he looked at the telephone. He had promised to tell Cellini of any new development, but he hated to tell the psychiatrist this. How could Dr. Cellini, Malleson, anyone, believe him in the face of such evidence? No wonder Tomlinson had been so convinced that he had lied! He actually touched the telephone, but drew his hand back quickly. The tautness at his head was back again, not severe but quite noticeable. Five minutes ago he would have thought it gone forever.

He scribbled a few notes on some of the letters, but his hand was unsteady and he could not think clearly. *Bertha would not lie;* he would as soon believe himself a liar. And if she had told the truth then he *had* talked with that youth, he *had* been up to Hilltop on that fateful afternoon.

He wiped his forehead again; it was very wet.

His telephone rang. He hesitated, but forced himself to pick it up.

"Yes?"

"Oh, Mr. Justin," Bertha said, "Mr. Malleson is coming over. He asked if you were in and I said you were."

"Thanks," said Justin. "That's all right." He put the receiver down and leaned back heavily.

If he looked like this when Malleson arrived it would be like a confession of guilt. He made himself get up and go to the upstairs washroom. He washed his face in cold water, then opened the window and looked out over the roundabout, the lawns, and the flower beds.

Malleson was here already, talking to the driver of the police car that had followed Justin from his apartment.

He could do with a drink, but it would be folly this early in the morning. Quite suddenly he realized what he must do. He snatched up the telephone and dialed Dr. Cellini's number. For a few moments he was on edge in case Malleson should come up the stairs, but Cellini answered before there was any sound from below.

"Dr. Cellini," Justin said, "I'm nearly back where I started from."

"I am very sorry to hear that," Cellini said, and the very sound of his voice was reassuring. "What has happened?" As Justin told him, the expected sounds came from below, and firm footsteps sounded on the stairs. "I *see*," Cellini went on. "That is quite remarkable, but I don't think it need distress you unduly. . . . Now I advise you to behave exactly as you *feel* with the inspector. . . . Don't put on an act of any kind."

Malleson was in the doorway, his face set, his eyes narrowed; his manner harsh and uncompromising.

". . . I repeat, behave exactly as you feel," Cellini was saying. "If you are frightened, don't try to hide it. . . . If you have tried to live by absolute truth, why do you try to desert it in a crisis?"

Justin actually laughed.

"That is much better! Please advise me as soon as you can as to why the inspector has come."

"I will," promised Justin. "Just as soon as I know."

He rang off and stood up. He might not cut a very impressive figure, but at least much of the tension had gone; Dr. Cellini was as good as a stiff brandy any time. He gave a half smile and motioned to a chair. Malleson sat down, but refused a cigarette. He looked tired, Justin thought: What happened when a policeman suffered from overstrain and domestic worries?

"Justin," Malleson said, "I don't know whether to believe a word you say, about anything."

"You've made that pretty obvious," said Justin dryly. "What do you think I've been lying about this time?" As he spoke he realized that a few days ago he could not have made that riposte so calmly. He was infinitely better in spite of the shock from Bertha.

Abruptly, Malleson said, "This woman, Charlotte Warwick."

"You don't doubt her existence, surely!"

"Oh, I don't doubt her existence. I'm not sure whether the name you gave is true or false, though. You've had no correspondence with her, have you?" The question was rhetorical, for he went on without a pause, "She does not live at the Outram Hotel, where you say you took her. Every household in Ringborn has been questioned and no one knows of a Charlotte Warwick. No one had a visitor recently who answered her description. So you lied to me about her, too."

Justin didn't speak; he could hardly think, the shock of this was so great.

He could remember, and *feel*—he could picture her in his mind's eye, serene and beautiful, so gay on the first day he had met her, so natural and frank. He hadn't enjoyed himself so much for years. And on the second day she had been different: harassing him, hoping to change his mind for him. . . .

"Well?" Malleson almost barked.

Justin said, "I can imagine how you feel, Eric. Can you"— he gulped—"can you imagine how I feel? I told you exactly and precisely what happened. She told me about herself and I passed everything she said on to you. So, she lied to me. Heaven knows why, but she lied to me."

Malleson stood up slowly, his expression hardening. "So that's your answer. *She* lied, not you."

"Yes," Justin said evenly. "I've told you the simple truth."

"Why should people lie? Why should your friends, even Bertha Briggs downstairs, people who wish you well—why should they lie and so condemn you to a charge of murder and all that will follow if you are found guilty? Can you explain that?" Malleson demanded, and then went on almost between his teeth, "If you can, I may have another excuse for not charging you."

Justin didn't speak.

"You're usually quick enough with your denials. What's happened?" Malleson was too tense, too sharp-voiced. "Are you going to admit the truth?"

"As far as I know, I always do," Justin said.

"As far as . . ." began Malleson, and then stopped short.

Justin's hands were pressing very tightly against his desk.

"Who were the other witnesses, apart from Bertha?" he asked.

"You can't expect me to tell you that," replied Malleson.

"Why not?" Justin demanded. "You've done some odd things in this investigation. Why stop now? Who were the people who saw me at Hilltop?"

Malleson drew a deep breath. "The Carmichaels," he said. "Husband and wife."

The Carmichaels, servants to the Pantanellis for fifty years, and absolutely reliable. They wouldn't lie; they might not like him, but they would not lie.

Malleson asked, quite softly, "Well, Justin?"

"Who else?" asked Justin stiffly.

"Peggy Nelson," answered Malleson very slowly.

Justin felt the blood draining from his cheeks. He didn't speak at once, but the tension was returning, and he felt sick. Peggy Nelson, with her merry eyes and her unspoken invitation, her moments of understanding. There was no reason in the world why she should be vindictive toward him. Bertha . . . the Carmichaels . . . Peggy Nelson. Oh God, it was unbelievable!

He uttered the names aloud, and then said thinly, "You couldn't disbelieve them."

"No. And I don't."

"So, I must have been at Hilltop."

"You were. Are you telling me you don't remember?"

"As far as I'm concerned I wasn't at Hilltop and I didn't talk to young Micky Jones about anything," Justin said. He dropped back into his chair. "I don't even know why I should. Are you going to charge me?"

"Justin."

"Yes?"

"I need one thing to prove my case."

"What is it?"

"Have you access to digitalin?"

"No," Justin said. "No. But Mrs. Pantanelli had. She had a supply in her bedroom." He caught his breath. "My God!" He remembered the talk with Dr. Cellini and James Tomlinson, and Tomlinson saying that whoever had injected the digitalin must have been unaware that her treatment with the drug had been discontinued. "She told me she didn't trust the new medicine, and had kept back a supply of digitalin and a syringe in case she had an attack and needed it desperately. The Carmichaels knew that. I knew it. Whoever gave her that overdose *didn't* know it."

Hope flared back, putting vigor into his voice, strength into his body.

"Can't you see that Eric? Can't you see it?"

"Yes," Malleson said, but he spoke without much enthusiasm. "For what it's worth, I see it." There was a long pause before he went on, "This woman, Charlotte Warwick."

"I've told you the truth about her. Good God, man, everyone knows she was here, I didn't dream her up. I took her to the Rose and Crown for dinner the first night, and drove her home. There was an Indian porter at the hotel. He'll remember. Have you checked the night staff?"

"No," Malleson said. "But I will. I'll need a photograph of you. Have you a good one?"

"No, sir, I'm sorry," the young porter said. "I know many people come and go, but I do not remember this man. I am sorry."

Justin woke soon after seven o'clock the next morning, feeling both tired and dispirited. He did not know the result of Malleson's inquiry; he did recall Malleson's lack of enthusiasm about the contention that the murderer could not have known of the change of treatment. He got up, made tea, shaved and bathed. Everything was normal, yet he felt a strong sense of impending disaster. He was making coffee when his telephone rang.

"Justin Gray," he said.

"Justin, this is Maurice," his cousin said briskly. "Will you be in this morning?"

"Yes," Justin answered.

"I'd like us all to meet at half-past ten," Maurice said. "Be there." He rang off.

Justin put the receiver down slowly. The toast sprang up in the toaster, but he did not remove it. He went to the window and looked out. It was a clear, sunlit morning, promising warmth. This had been a rare and lovely summer. He watched two thrushes perched on a branch, heads held back as if feeling superiority over all they saw, just as Maurice had sounded.

Maurice hadn't made a request, he had issued a command: "Be there."

He, Justin, would be there. No matter how much he disliked Maurice, he must be there, because he owed an explanation to his cousins. He ate his toast and marmalade mechanically, and the food seemed to have little taste.

Why should anyone do these things to him? Why send those dogs, lure those bees, leave the sparrow on his desk?

He hadn't arranged any part of it. It made no difference what Bertha, Peggy, or the Carmichaels said. He had not organized that campaign against himself; it was cunningly, skillfully conceived to drive him crazy.

No, no one could be sure it would turn his mind.

Then what?

To drive him out of the business?

Good God! Was that it?

"Yes, that has to be considered," said Dr. Cellini. "It might be assumed that Maurice wishes to be free of you, and after your refusal to compromise, set this plan in action. You have been . . . ah . . . summoned for ten-thirty, you say."

"Yes."

"See them," Dr. Cellini advised. "Be wholly yourself with them. If you feel like breaking Maurice's neck, make your feelings obvious. Be yourself, Justin, wholly yourself."

"I'll be myself," Justin promised grimly. "Dr. Cellini."

"Yes?"

"Can I believe *you?*"

"I think you can accept my good will and my integrity absolutely," said Cellini. "What makes you ask that question?"

"I want a true answer to another."

"Yes?"

"Am I mad?" asked Justin, very harshly.

"You are not mad at all," Dr. Cellini assured him with quiet, convincing emphasis. "You are hated—that is the simple truth. And I do not believe there is any serious doubt that the man who hates you is your cousin Maurice. I will join you in Hodenham as soon as I can, certainly no later than two o'clock this afternoon. The one thing I demand of you is that you be yourself. If you feel like losing your temper, lose it. If you feel like accusing your cousin, accuse him. Even if you feel so infuriated that you are tempted to use physical violence, use it.

"Be yourself, Justin, in every way."

Chapter 17

"I AM MYSELF"

THEY WERE all three waiting for him in the board room. There was one significant difference. The place at the table in front of the window, usually his, was already taken—by Maurice. Since they had worked together that had been Justin's place, as chairman for the year. He made no comment, but looked at them each in turn.

Alan was uneasy and unable to meet his eye; usually untidy, he appeared to be a little too sleekly groomed. Hugo sat impressively, hands on the table, fingers linked. Soon his hands would begin to move, clenching and unclenching as his nervousness and his indecision increased—if, today, he had not come with his mind fully made up.

Maurice looked more decisive, the big head, the dark brown eyes, the thick dark eyebrows as boldly drawn as features in a portrait.

Alan cleared his throat; none of the others spoke.

Justin felt a calmness that he knew had come out of the talk with Cellini. "Be yourself," Cellini seemed to be whispering to him. "Lose your temper . . . accuse your cousin . . . use physical violence." He stood in the doorway, looking from one to the other, and then strode toward Maurice. As his cousin twisted around, he heaved him from the chair, then, still without a word, quietly took his accustomed place.

"What the hell are you doing!" gasped Alan.

"Taking my usual place," Justin answered simply.

"My God!" breathed Maurice. "I'll kill you for this!"

He was glaring. His fists were tightly clenched. His jacket

was rucked up about his waist and his shoulders. His eyes were blazing, as if he were internally on fire.

"Sit down and stop talking nonsense," Justin said. "You've already tried to prove me a liar and a murderer, and you've failed. What do you want now?"

Hugo sprang up. "Maurice, don't!" he cried. "Maurice!"

Maurice had raised the back of a chair as if it were a weapon; he was capable of smashing it down on Justin's head. Justin did not move. Hugo closed with Maurice, gripping the chair, tugging at it. Alan half rose to his feet, darting glances from Maurice to Justin and back again.

"You . . . you are a liar!" he gasped.

"Neither liar nor murderer," Justin said equably, "but capable of wringing Maurice's neck if he doesn't sit down and stop making a fool of himself."

Now Alan's gaze was all for Justin; as if he were mesmerized.

"For God's sake sit down!" Hugo gasped.

Slowly, Maurice let go of the chair. He did not look away from Justin but allowed himself to be half led, half pushed, toward the empty side of the table and the chair in front of it. Justin felt the sudden heat of reaction. Had Cellini known that he would? He had established an ascendancy that he had to maintain; it shouldn't be difficult, for they were used to a stubborn, defensive attitude from him.

Maurice sat down, breathing through clenched teeth.

"Now let's have it," Justin said.

Maurice didn't speak. Hugo sat down and his fingers began to flex and unflex.

"We . . . we had just voted you out of the firm."

"Well, I've just voted myself in again."

"You . . . you *can't!*" muttered Alan.

"We don't have a written deed of agreement, we don't have articles, we don't have any kind of formal partnership," Justin said. "So we fall back on precedent each time. We meet on the first Monday in January every year and choose a chairman. That's when I'll go."

"You'll be in jail before then," sneered Maurice. His voice was pitched high and he still found it difficult to breathe easily. "Do you think we're going to be ordered about by a stinking hypocrite and a cold-blooded killer? If you do, you're mistaken."

It was almost funny; it *was* funny. Justin laughed.

"Everything will be as democratic as ever," he said. "Is this why you called the meeting?"

"Justin, be reasonable," Hugo said. It was possible to hear his fingers sliding against one another, and there was a beading of sweat on his forehead. "In view of what's happened, of the suspicion, we *can't* have you . . . have you active in the business any longer. If you hadn't been so . . . if you hadn't assaulted Maurice we would have told you what we propose. It's no use losing our tempers over this."

"I haven't lost my temper . . . yet," Justin said.

"You're so damned aggressive."

"Yes," agreed Justin, "you could call it that. I'm angry, and I'm sick to death of the lot of you. What do you propose?"

"They're very reasonable proposals," Alan muttered.

"Suppose you tell me what they are," suggested Justin.

Hugo glanced past him, out of the window. Alan stared at Maurice, the spokesman. Even Maurice hesitated before he said:

"We'll buy you out—for cash—provided you leave Hodenham."

"Oh," said Justin heavily. "Buy me out, or rather, drive me out. Is that it?"

"You can think yourself damned lucky," Maurice said. "After this, you'll never be able to show your face in Hodenham again—in England, for that matter. We'll put up part of the cash now—you'll need it as far as I can see, to pay for your defense. And the balance will be waiting for you."

"When I come out of jail. Is that it?"

"That's right," Maurice said. "When you come out of prison. The only thing that will get you off is an insanity plea, and no one will ever believe you're insane. Just that you're a congenital liar and humbug who has been fooling the whole district for years."

"I see," said Justin. "You're very sure I'm going to be convicted, aren't you?"

"It's all over the town—*every*one knows," Hugo said deliberately. He was acting a part now, even his voice changed. "The remarkable thing is that you haven't been charged yet. It can only be a matter of time."

"Possibly," Justin said. "But until that time comes I'm as free as you are. And as for the business—my answer is no. I'm not interested in selling."

"But Justin—" Alan began.

"But nothing," said Justin sharply. "A quarter of this business is mine, and it's going to stay mine. And while I'm at liberty to make sure, the business will be run honestly and decently."

"*Honestly!*" cried Hugo. "That's the joke of the year!"

"You've been waiting until you could get your hands on the whole of the Pantanelli property so as to make a killing, and you still talk of honesty!" Maurice sneered. "You nauseate me."

"I know exactly how you feel," Justin said. "You've had that effect on me for a long time. And it's particularly strong now. I don't know how you've done it but I do know you have cleverly built up a campaign to present me as a liar and a murderer to drive me out of the business and out of Hoden-

ham. You, Maurice—no one else unless these hangers-on of
yours have helped you with it. But it won't succeed. Only a
fool would even think it had a hope of success."

White-faced, Maurice said, "There isn't a word of truth in
what you're saying."

"Think again."

"There's no need. Bertha *saw* you. The Carmichaels *saw*
you. Even Peggy Nelson, who'd jump into bed with you if you
raised so much as a finger, had to admit the truth!" Maurice
stood up and for the first time there was something like dignity in his manner. "Sooner or later the bad blood between us
had to come out into the open. I've always believed you were
a fraud. Now I bloody well know you are and so does everyone else."

He turned and stalked out of the room.

Alan half rose, and then dropped back into his chair.

"Justin, old chap," said Hugo, slipping expertly into another role, "why don't you see reason? You don't like the business, that's very obvious. I don't agree with Maurice, I don't
think you're a fraud, but I do think you're . . . you're too
good for the hurly-burly business of today. You can't *be*
honest in the way you try to be—the rules beat you all the
time. Business is a jungle, old man. You weren't meant to live
in a jungle."

"Hugo's right," said Alan eagerly. "This isn't the work you
ought to be doing. We're tuned to it, you aren't. So let's buy
you out. I don't believe you killed Mrs. P.; Maurice always
goes too far, but he's right about the firm. There isn't room
for the two of you in this business. For your own sake, Justin,
accept the offer. You'll never regret it."

Justin stood up, looked from one to the other, and said
scathingly, "Of the three of you, I think I prefer Maurice."

He went out.

He was halfway down the stairs when he felt giddy, missed

a step, and then grabbed the handrail to save himself. Bertha passed the foot of the stairs, but did not look up. Justin went hot and cold, and his nerves began to quiver, and the tightness in his head came back. It was reaction, of course—reaction to his own onslaught, to what Maurice had said, to the attitude of the others—even to the fact that they seemed to take it for granted that he would be accused and tried.

All his doubts and fears came flooding back.

He went out, walking slowly toward the side street where he had parked his car. Two men in a police car were across the road, making no secret of their interest in him. Someone, a woman, was following him, and she drew level with him. He dropped heavily into the driving seat, but did not immediately touch the wheel.

"Justin . . . are you all right?"

It was Peggy Nelson, yet he hadn't recognized her when he had seen her approaching the car.

He didn't answer; he felt too strained, too hopeless.

"Where are you going?" she asked. "Home?"

He nodded.

"Move over, I'll drive you," she said briskly.

He obeyed, knowing that he could no more drive safely than if he was drunk. It was a bench seat, and the gear was on the handle; sliding across was easy enough. Peggy drove with easy confidence; up to now it had always been he who had driven her. Vaguely he was aware that he had not even known that she could drive.

She pulled up outside his front door.

"Is your door key one of these?" She took the keys out of the ignition.

"The gold-colored one," Justin muttered.

"Can you manage by yourself?" she asked. "I'll open the door."

She got out, young and lissome, with long, shapely legs, and while he was fumbling with the handle she opened the door and stretched an arm toward him. He caught hold of it, glad of the support, but it was an effort to get up the stairs. She steadied him to his armchair, and then opened the cupboard where he kept his liquor. Without a word, she poured brandy and brought it to him.

He sipped, and felt the warmth stealing soothingly through his body. She moved back and stood staring down at him. There was nothing remotely mischievous in her eyes or in her manner. She was as stern-faced as he could remember, rather like an earnest schoolmistress.

"You shouldn't be alone so much," she said.

"I . . . daresay you're right."

"I am right. And I am *not* suggesting that you should live with me, in case you get any wrong ideas. You need people— company. Someone who doesn't think you're crazy, too."

He felt better; not right, but better. In a mild way she affected him as Dr. Cellini had.

"You mean *you* don't think I'm crazy?"

"Oh, I do. I think you're banging your head against a brick wall with those cousins of yours; all three put together aren't worth your little finger. Would you like to tell me what happened this morning?"

"My cousins don't think I'm good for the business."

"I don't think I want to talk about your cousins," Peggy said. "But perhaps I will. Hugo, of course, is the wolf of Hodenham. Alan is a would-be wolf—how his wife stands it, I don't know. Maurice—no, I *won't* tell you what I think of Maurice." She paused, hands on her hips. "Did you have any breakfast?"

"Er . . . yes."

"Toast and coffee?"

"Well . . ."

"I'll make you an omelette," she said briskly. "Sit back and relax. More brandy?"

"No, thanks," he said quite firmly.

He would ask her to tell him exactly when she had seen him, where he was supposed to have been, when she came back. She was nice and very self-possessed. Efficient, too. He watched as she went off into the kitchen, and he remembered that she had been here to cocktail parties once or twice, and an occasional meeting of a subcommittee of the museum. He dozed. It wasn't surprising that his cousins were behaving as they were, and it wasn't even hurtful. The surprising thing was the way he had behaved. Even the danger of arrest, the fact that there might be some truth in what the trio had said, did not depress him. And it was pleasant to have Peggy about. Pleasant. He was dozing. He heard a sound at the door, but didn't open his eyes. She would come in when she was ready, he didn't have to wake himself.

Supposing the police *did* arrest him. It wasn't possible that a jury would convict him. Was it? Surely not. Anyhow, there was Dr. Cellini. And Tomlinson. The accusing figure of James Tomlinson—friend turned foe. Why had Tomlinson behaved like that? Was he still—of course, Dr. Cellini had said he was still well-disposed.

He heard voices.

He heard Dr. Cellini saying, "I do understand, Miss Nelson, but I really must see him. It is essential, even though you have to wake him. I understand that Inspector Malleson will be here in ten or fifteen minutes and I need to talk to Justin before he arrives."

Chapter 18

"ANYTHING YOU SAY
MAY BE USED . . ."

Dr. Cellini was at the open door; Peggy Nelson was just in front of him. Justin sat up and rubbed his eyes. His mouth was dry and his head heavy. When she saw he was awake, Peggy turned and went out—he was surprised and rather disturbed that she didn't say a word.

Cellini came forward. "A very pleasant young woman," he remarked. "Justin, how did the meeting with your cousins go?"

Justin sat upright. "I let *myself* go," he answered. "And afterward . . ."

"Afterward you had a reaction—of course you did. Hasn't it dawned on you yet that you *are* a sick man, that to get back to full health you need at least six months without any crises and problems?" Cellini pulled up a chair and sat down. "Tell me everything in your own words."

"Didn't I hear you say that Malleson's coming?"

"Yes," answered the older man.

The touch of his hand on Justin's shoulder was firm and light, his expression unworried.

"If he makes a charge you may be held at the police station, and come up before the magistrates in the morning. You would be remanded for a week, in the normal course of events, and I might not be able to talk to you as freely as I can now."

So Cellini expected him to be charged with murder. There could be no other explanation of his urgency.

Justin drew a deep breath.

"Very well," he said. "Maurice was sitting in my chair, and I tossed him out. He was quite venomous. They had planned to buy me out of the business, and I was condemned as hypocrite, fraud, and murderer. Hugo and Alan were slippery. Maurice did at least say exactly what he thought. I accused him of plotting this against me, with or without the others' help. I took the initiative and managed to keep it until I left. Then I nearly cracked up. Peggy . . . was at hand. She brought me here."

"I know what happened from the time you got here," said Cellini. "That young woman is as lucid as she is likable. Now, when Malleson comes, do exactly as you did with your cousins. Be yourself. He is a police officer, not a judge. In some ways he has been overfriendly, in others oversevere. I can tell you that he has been in close contact with his chief superintendent, naturally he doesn't intend to put a foot wrong if he can help it. But nothing you do or say to him can affect the ultimate issue. He may imply that it can, but it cannot. Understand, Justin—be yourself."

"Why are you so insistent on that?" demanded Justin.

"Did it succeed this morning?"

"Yes, but . . ."

"It will succeed again if you allow yourself to be guided by your feelings, by your instincts. You have exercised a rigid self-control for too long, and it has taken a great deal out of you. Relax. Act on impulse. You are never likely to do a wrong thing instinctively and it doesn't matter if you sometimes lose your temper. Now—"

There was a ring at the front door bell.

"There they are," Justin said grimly. He moved toward the door, but Cellini stopped him.

"Peggy will let them in," he said. "Wait here for them."

Justin moistened his lips as Cellini moved toward the window, where the midday light shone on his face and his now silvery hair and gave him a kind of radiance. Looking at him, Justin felt a strange impression: there was a saintliness about this man, an ethereal quality. He was aware of Peggy hurrying—almost scampering—down the stairs, voices, then of heavy footsteps coming up. He knew that at least two men were there, and was as sure as he could be that it was Malleson and another, come to charge him. Yet he could not look away from Cellini, and he felt as calm as when he had stepped into the board room.

"Dr. Cellini."

"Yes?"

"They would not charge me unless they were sure they had convincing evidence."

"That is quite right."

"Mr. Tomlinson seemed to find the evidence convincing."

"He was trying to shake your story, trying to make you break down if you were in fact lying," Cellini told him. "He failed. You were most convincing under the pressure he exerted. Don't worry about Tomlinson."

The men outside were on the landing now; and Malleson spoke to Peggy as Cellini's voice faded.

"Which room?" Malleson asked abruptly.

"The front room—there," Peggy answered.

"Supposing the jury believes the evidence?" Justin asked in a breathless voice.

"Then you would be convicted," Cellini said simply. "But if you didn't do it, the evidence will not be sufficient to condemn you."

There was a tap at the door, sharp and peremptory.

"Yes?" Cellini called.

"There have been . . . miscarriages of justice," Justin said tautly. "This could be another."

"*Mr. Gray! Open the door, please!*"

"It could indeed," began Dr. Cellini. "But—"

"Do you think they will believe the evidence as we know it?" Justin caught his breath.

"*Mr. Gray!*"

"Why don't you open the door and go in?" Peggy asked in an acid voice.

The door opened and Malleson appeared, but Justin did not look at him, he was so intent on what Cellini was saying.

"I cannot believe any of those witnesses could lie," Cellini went on. "So why should the jury think them liars?"

"Mr. Gray," Malleson said in a quieter voice. "I wish to talk to you in confidence, please."

Behind Malleson was another man in plainclothes, and behind him, Peggy, on tiptoe—anxious and angrily bright-eyed. Malleson still looked tired, but also solid and powerful and quite sure of himself.

"You can say what you like in front of Dr. Cellini," Justin said. "Have you met Inspector Malleson, Dr. Cellini?"

"Very briefly," said Cellini. "Good afternoon, Inspector."

"Good afternoon, sir." Malleson hardly glanced at him. "Mr. Gray, I would like you to come with me to the police station to help us with our inquiries into the death of Mrs. Louise Pantanelli." Malleson's eyes seemed to add, *Don't make it worse for yourself by making a fuss.*

"Can't I help you here?" Justin asked quickly.

"Not satisfactorily, no."

"Then I'm afraid whatever you get from me must be unsat-isfactory," Justin said.

"*Hear, hear!*" Peggy breathed.

"I don't understand you," said Malleson.

"I'll gladly answer any questions you like here," said Justin. "But not at the police station."

Malleson, obviously taken aback, glanced at Cellini, then back to Justin, who was amazed at his own calmness and complete control of the situation.

"Just . . ." Malleson began, and quickly recovered himself. "I must ask you to come with me at once, Mr. Gray."

"Not of my own free will," Justin said.

Malleson squared his shoulders, cleared his throat, and said in a very hoarse voice:

"I ask you once more, Mr. Gray, to come with me to the police station to help us with our inquiries."

"And once more, I refuse," replied Justin.

"In that case . . ." Malleson hesitated, cleared his throat again, and then asked what appeared to be an absurd question. "Is your name Justin Gray?"

"Yes," answered Justin flatly.

"*You know it is,*" said Peggy, in exasperation.

"Be quiet, miss, please." Malleson paused, and drew a deep breath. "Mr. Gray, it is my duty to charge you that on the nineteenth day of June in this year of grace you did unlawfully administer to Mrs. Louise Pantanelli an injection of digitalin knowing that it would cause her death. I must warn you that anything you say will be taken down and may be used as evidence."

Very deliberately, Justin said, "I have nothing to say."

"You are required now to accompany me to the police station, there to be taken into custody until you may plead before a magistrate," went on Malleson.

"Very well," said Justin.

Peggy had gone very white. Justin smiled at her faintly. The second plainclothesman came forward, and Malleson moved to one side.

"Follow Detective Sergeant Smith, please."

Justin moved toward Smith, who went out onto the landing and started down the stairs. Malleson stepped close behind him. Going down the stairs in military precision had something almost comical about it. Even when he saw a uniformed policeman by the front door, another by the gate, Justin was not as impressed as he might have been. Once they were in the street, it was another matter. He saw Malleson's car, with the driver at the wheel, his own car parked nearby—and at least thirty people being kept back from the path by half a dozen policemen. Three photographers, men he knew well, were at the front of the crowd, and cameras clicked. Reporters were standing by; one man was talking into a tape recorder while a long-haired youth next to him used a ciné camera on a tripod.

Why hadn't he expected something like this? *Why hadn't he been warned?*

The reporter was saying into his microphone:

"Justin Gray is being led from the front gate of his house by Chief Inspector Malleson, officer in charge of the Hodenham Subdivisional Police Station. . . . Gray is looking straight ahead, a tall, distinguished-looking man. Behind him is . . ."

Justin ducked to get into the police car. He felt a sudden attack of dizziness, and stumbled. Malleson, just behind him, grabbed and steadied him, and he flopped down into the corner. He began to tremble, and knew the blood was draining from his face. Suddenly the car seemed to be surrounded by a mass of people, blurred, pressed close to the window. A youth screeched:

"Murderer!"

Someone else shouted, "They ought to bring back the rope!"

"Murderer!"

"What harm did she ever do you?"

Policemen began to push the crowd away. A car moved off

in front of the one in which Justin was sitting beside Malleson, the detective sergeant by the side of the driver.

"Hang him!" a youth screamed. "Hang him!"

Justin sat back, utterly helpless, utterly despairing, with no strength in him at all. His head drooped, his chin was on his chest. One hand rested on his knee, the other hung loosely, over the edge of his seat. Malleson stared at him, but Justin was hardly aware of it.

"You bloody fool, why didn't you give yourself a break?" Malleson asked, almost savagely. Justin did not answer. "Once we've charged you, you've become public property. I've done all I possibly can to help you—and you have to let yourself be bluffed by that old fool Cellini."

That—old—fool—Cellini.

That—old—fool—

That—old—

His head was swimming, and he seemed to be floating in air.

"That old fool Cellini—be yourself, be yourself, be yourself—that old fool—"

"Justin! Stop it! For God's sake stop it!"

That old fool—be yourself—hang him—murderer—old fool—what harm has she ever done you?—they ought to bring back the rope—

"*Justin!*"

He felt Malleson's hands on his shoulders and realized that he was shaking violently, teeth chattering, body going up and down. The car turned a corner and threw him against the window; he banged his head, almost without knowing it. But gradually the shaking eased, and soon he sat back limply, perspiration breaking out all over his body. Malleson released him.

"Better?" he asked gruffly.

"I'm . . . all right."

"You had me scared."

"I . . . had *you* scared!" Justin managed to mutter.

"Should you see a doctor?"

"All I need is . . . to rest for a bit."

"Smith," Malleson said to the sergeant, "arrange for a doctor to be at the station as soon as possible."

"Right, sir." Smith picked up a radio-telephone.

"Thanks," Justin muttered. "But I'll be all right."

"What happened to you? Are . . . good God!"

"What's the matter?"

"Er . . . forget it."

If Malleson wanted to forget what had made him exclaim, Justin had no objection. He was only too glad to sit back and listen to Smith calling for the doctor. He hoped it wouldn't be Nash.

What had made Malleson break off so suddenly? . . . Oh, forget it! as Malleson had said.

He was glad when they reached the station, glad that he wasn't immediately taken down to the cells; he had visited prisoners there several times. Instead, Malleson took him to a small waiting room and left him in an armchair, watched over by a policeman who looked scarcely old enough to be out of school.

He half dozed, all tension gone, a kind of numbness in its place.

Malleson spoke quietly into the telephone in his office.

"He wouldn't come on a request, sir, so I had to charge him. He was completely composed and normal when I saw him, but collapsed as soon as he got into the car. The change was quite remarkable—so remarkable that I think we should have him medically examined. He knows I've sent for a doctor."

"You certainly need a doctor," the divisional superintendent approved. "I've just had Mr. Tomlinson on the line. He's sending over a medical certificate stating that Justin Gray is suffering from acute nervous exhaustion and should be allowed to rest. We'll need our man to state he's fit to plead in the morning. Who are your local chaps?"

"Nash and Osmond."

"Don't use either," urged the superintendent. "I'll send Dr. Prendergast over. If we put him up, no one is going to get away with anything, and he won't let anyone bully him in court. You say Cellini was with Gray at his home?"

"Yes, sir. He seems to have a remarkable effect on Gray."

"Before you let Cellini see him again, let me know," ordered the superintendent. "Cellini has a remarkable effect on a lot of people. I wish I knew what his interest was in this case. Is there anything else on your mind?" He changed the subject abruptly.

"I've been trying to think what could affect Gray like this—absolutely on top one minute, and down to rock bottom the next," said Malleson. "Had it been a kid, young Micky Joncs for instance, I would have jumped to one possibility at once. It didn't occur to me with Gray until five minutes ago."

"Are you suggesting drugs?" demanded the superintendent.

"It would answer a lot of questions, wouldn't it?" asked Malleson.

"It certainly would," the senior man agreed. "Tell Prendergast the symptoms, but don't mention drugs. He won't miss it, if that's the explanation."

Chapter 19

THE NEED OF
JUSTIN GRAY

Dr. Emmanuel Cellini stood at the window of Justin Gray's flat and watched him being taken away, noticing how his legs seemed to bend under him. He heard Peggy Nelson exclaim in alarm. He did not touch the girl, but looked at her gravely. She dashed her hand across her eyes—to clear her vision, he thought, not because she was ashamed of crying.

The cars moved off. The shouting sounded loud and clear.

"*Murderer!*"

"*They ought to bring back the rope.*"

"*What did she ever do to you?*"

Peggy rose to tiptoe as the police cars neared the end of the street, then swung past a shop on the corner and disappeared. For the first time she turned to Cellini, and saw that he was studying her.

"Well, he did what you told him," she said huskily. "I hope it doesn't send him to prison."

"I won't send him to prison," Cellini said. "The evidence could."

She asked bitterly, "Are you suggesting that I should have lied to the police? I *saw* him. There's no question about that. I hate the thought that *my* evidence might make things worse for him, but—" She broke off.

"You would do the same again," Cellini murmured.

"I would *have* to! Surely you can see that."

"Yes," agreed Cellini, with obvious satisfaction. "Will you

make some coffee, my dear? I'll come and talk to you as you make it, if I may." As they went into the old-fashioned kitchen, he added, "Instant coffee will do, of course."

"It's all I can make, so it will have to." Peggy put on an electric kettle with marked concentration. "What do you think will happen to him?"

"I'm more concerned with what I think *should* happen," replied Cellini. "And with what I have been trying to do with Justin. I've been trying to teach him the lesson he has almost forgotten."

"Oh, what's the use of standing there and talking about teaching him lessons? He's just been charged with murder!"

"So it is more important than ever that he comes to terms with his very special quality," said Cellini.

"His—*what?*"

"His special—his almost unique—quality. He is nearer than anyone I know to being a selfless man, but no one can subjugate himself entirely. He has tried to. We are all human beings, all have weaknesses, and sooner or later we all have to indulge them. If we don't, we chip away a little of our humanity, make ourselves a little less human than we are. Justin has been chipping away at his for many years."

The kettle was singing; Peggy was staring at Cellini, her eyes intent, as if at last she was beginning to understand what he was saying.

"The essential thing is to be self-indulgent in a way that does harm neither to oneself nor to others," Cellini said. "A simple way is to have someone in whom to confide. How long have you known him?"

"Most of my life," Peggy answered.

"How long have you loved him?" asked Cellini gently.

She did not attempt to deny that she did, hesitated only for a few seconds, and then said:

"Most of my life, too, I suppose. But he's been . . . almost unapproachable."

"Did you know the young woman, Moira?"

"I knew her better than I knew him, I think," answered Peggy, and with strange intensity went on. "She was absolutely right for him."

"And the accident condemned him to loneliness," said Cellini. "Have you ever succeeded in getting through to Justin, past the defenses with which he unconsciously surrounds himself?"

"No," she answered. "I don't think he sees me as a woman at all. To him I am merely a schoolgirl to be given boxes of chocolates at birthdays and Christmas—oh, what is the use of *talking?*" She spun around, searched the shelves for a cream jug, put everything on a tray, and carried it past Cellini into the living room.

"It could matter a lot," Cellini answered thoughtfully. "I think you are making the same mistake as he is, Peggy. You think the important factor in this case is whether he is tried for murder and whether he is found guilty. You are wrong, my dear."

"That sounds to me suspiciously like nonsense," she cried.

Cellini shrugged his shoulders expressively. "The important thing in this case is whether he can lose the tensions that his self-discipline has created. If he can, then there could be a great future in front of him. He has both a good mind— almost unused so far—and remarkable principles. Let him be humanized by emotion, indeed by love, and he will be a far, far happier man."

She handed him his coffee, as if not realizing what she was doing.

"I don't understand you. If he stands trial, if he's found guilty, it will ruin him!"

"Some of our greatest men have been through fire before finding their greatness," Cellini said. "Some of the world's leaders spent years in prison, and it toughened, not weakened, them. Good men come through a time of testing, and are not broken by it."

"You don't seem to care what happens to him," Peggy said bitterly.

"Indeed, I care. I care a great deal. I began to do so when Mr. Tomlinson first told me about Justin."

"Tomlinson did! But he's such a pedantic old man!"

"And I am often judged a fussy one," said Cellini wryly. "James Tomlinson is a remarkable man in his way, one of the most observant I have known. He told me that he had been watching Justin for some years, and had even contemplated asking me to meet him—had in fact planned that we should meet when the museum committee put my little collection of gold on display. He had seen a crisis pending, but only in normal terms, not under such pressure as the last few days. And he told me that he thought Maurice Mendelson was almost as evil as his cousin was good—but not dedicated to evil as such, only to getting his own way."

"Amazing! I'd no idea Mr. Tomlinson thought along those lines."

"He is extremely anxious to help Justin. He is in fact going to see the police this afternoon, and will arrange to see Justin and to act for him."

"I can hardly believe it," Peggy said. "I thought—" She broke off.

"Please go on."

"I thought Justin was so alone that no one could really get near him."

"This has been the problem," said Cellini. "The fence of unapproachability—not of his own deliberate making, but almost inevitable in view of his attitudes. He has lived by, and insisted on, standards which few people could achieve, and because of that they have kept aloof from him. And as he couldn't get through to people, couldn't communicate because they appeared to have different values, he withdrew more into himself."

"I should have tried more," Peggy said woefully.

"You would have been most ill-advised," Cellini said firmly. "It would have lent a cheapness to the relationship that you would never have lived down. As time progresses and the relationship between the sexes becomes more natural and less artificial, no doubt humanity will greatly benefit. But we live in today's world. The only people who really have any culpability for Justin's troubles are his cousins. Maurice and Justin were natural enemies. The other two could have helped had they been stronger, or better, characters but they took Maurice's side simply because they thought it would make them more money."

"Do you mean actively?"

"Oh yes," said Cellini. "They were active enough. I have no doubt at all that the plot to drive him out of the business has been developing for some time. Certainly it couldn't have been arranged at short notice. What puzzles—let me be honest, what *troubles* me—is the death of Mrs. Pantanelli. She *was* murdered. I have considered the possibility that it was a mercy killing—that Justin did in fact do it. But—"

"Oh no!" gasped Peggy. "He wouldn't have done that!"

"But I have rejected it," went on Cellini, pausing to sip his coffee, which was now quite cool. "If it had been a mercy killing, Justin would have said so. He would not have lied. Peggy, did you *really* see Justin heading for Hilltop?"

"Of course I did! I wish to heaven I hadn't!"

"How far away were you?"

"About a hundred yards, but I'd recognize him anywhere. I'd been out to see a friend, and saw Justin turning into the drive. I *saw* him, I know I did. And I'll have to swear to it in court."

"Yes," said Cellini. "You may have to very soon, perhaps tomorrow. Mr. Tomlinson believes it would be wise to call all the witnesses then, rather than accept a remand in custody. Are you free for the rest of the day?" he asked abruptly.

"Yes. If it will help Justin I'll be free for months!"

"Then this is what I want you to do . . ." said Cellini.

While Dr. Cellini was talking to Peggy Nelson, Dr. Cyril Prendergast, one of the most valued consultants to the Metropolitan Police, was examining Justin. Malleson was in his office going through the transcript of what had happened when he had been to see Gray and had finally charged him. It was an excellent transcript; Smith had even included the shouts of "Hang him!" "Murderer!" "What has she ever done to you?" The only dialogue not noted down was what he had said to Gray in the car.

Then he went over every report again.

The evidence of Micky Jones was not important, except that it appeared to prove Gray a liar. The fact that the will had been stolen the night before the murder was of itself puzzling—but it could be argued that Gray had wanted to check the contents and when he had reassured himself that he was the chief beneficiary, had decided to put the old soul away quickly. The motive, the large inheritance, the opportunity—all he needed as circumstantial evidence was there in the reports. But why had Gray been careless enough to leave the will in his flat?

Malleson heard footsteps outside and sprang up as Divisional Superintendent Endicott came in. Endicott was massive, graying, amiable-looking, well-dressed. No one was with him.

He shook hands.

"I didn't expect you, sir," Malleson said.

"An unexpected pleasure, eh?" said Endicott dryly. He sat down. "I wanted to have a word with Dr. Prendergast himself, as well as with you." He looked at the mass of typewritten reports. "Anything new in?"

"Nothing significant, as far as I can see," answered Malleson. He handed over the latest transcripts. "If I could explain why Gray kept the will in his flat, I wouldn't worry so much."

"H'mm." Endicott was skimming through the transcript. "H'mm!" he repeated, with much more vehemence. He tossed the transcript back. "What you want is all in there."

Malleson stared. "But I know that by heart!"

"Then you know that Gray suffers from these collapses, and that they come quite suddenly. All those we've known about have come after he's keyed himself up to make some special effort, but how do we know that he doesn't go through these crises when he's on his own? In fact, Eric, if he got that will and discovered for the first time that he was going to inherit a hundred thousand pounds, that could have brought on a reaction that made him push the will behind the furniture."

Malleson said huskily, "I'd missed that completely, sir."

"Yes, I know. You're taking this case very much to heart. I didn't realize you knew Gray as well as you do." Endicott leaned forward, to emphasize his point. "There's no need for you to see it through tomorrow. I can easily arrange for someone else to give the evidence of arrest, and stand in for you."

"Very good of you, sir," said Malleson stiffly, "but I would rather see it through myself. That is, if you've no objection, of course."

"Suit yourself," said Endicott. "I—"

There was a tap at the door.

"Dr. Prendergast, sir."

Prendergast was tall, very thin, with shiny skin stretched over sharp cheekbones. He moved loosely, as if he did not have absolute control of his muscles, but nothing could have been further from the truth.

His brown eyes lit up at the sight of Endicott.

"Hello, Fred." He shook hands with the superintendent. "Couldn't leave this alone, then!"

"Happened to be passing," Endicott said with a grin.

"Tell that to the Marines!" Prendergast sat on a corner of Malleson's desk, and went on, "A straightforward case of nervous exhaustion in a highly sensitive man. Nothing more. I'll take a look at his heart if you like, but I don't think it's necessary. If he could take it easy for a while, he'd be a very fit man. He might even benefit from a few weeks in prison before his trial." Prendergast turned back to Endicott. "Sure you've got him?"

"Yes, we've got him," Endicott answered. "He was at the house. He's got the most powerful motive in the world— money. He was there often enough to know where the digitalin was. Oh yes, Chief Inspector Malleson's done a very good job."

"Just one thing, Doctor," Malleson said diffidently.

"Yes?"

"These collapses of Gray's—could they be brought on by any sustained excitement or period of tension?"

"Yes."

"Is there any possibility of his using drugs?"

"I can find no evidence at all," answered Prendergast. "Whose idea was that?"

"Er . . . I just wondered, sir. Supposing he'd stolen this will, and discovered he benefited by a hundred thousand pounds. Would that have been enough to bring on an attack?"

"More than enough," Prendergast answered.

"Then we *have* got him," declared Endicott. "Even Cellini and Tomlinson together can't get him out of this now."

They both looked at Malleson.

"It's a queer thing," Malleson said. "From the beginning, I thought Justin was lying, I had all the proof I needed, and yet at the same time I couldn't really believe him capable of murder. And I still can't," he added. He stood up abruptly. "Shall we give formal evidence of arrest and ask for an eight-day remand in custody, sir?"

"Yes," said Endicott. "But have witnesses subpoenaed. We might need to put up a case, if Tomlinson thinks it will help his client. We may need you, Cyril. Can you stand by?"

"If need be," Prendergast said. "I'll tell you what."

"What?"

"Cellini will probably be put up as an expert witness to state that Gray isn't fit to plead, and ask for him to be sent for medical examination. Get a psychiatrist to look him over. He *is* fit to plead, but to outwit one psychiatrist you will need another."

"I'll arrange that, Eric," Endicott promised.

Another doctor, thought Justin. Well, it made little difference. He felt quite composed, despite examinations by two doctors, two visits from Tomlinson, several from Malleson, one from a man whose name he didn't catch but which ended in "cott."

He did not see or hear from Cellini, or from Peggy Nelson.

He would have liked to talk to Peggy, confident that she wouldn't argue, wouldn't try to talk him into compromise as Charlotte Warwick had. She wasn't beautiful, she hadn't Charlotte's vitality and gift of words, but she was kind, and bright, and gay.

Kind . . .

And tomorrow he would be accused in court of having murdered dear, trusting old Louise Pantanelli.

Chapter 20

THE WITNESSES

THE LAST TIME Justin had been in the courtroom had been as a witness in a case of mortgage foreclosure. He had tried to prevent a mortgage from foreclosing and evicting a man who had tried to maintain his payments but had failed. He had failed, too.

This morning the court was jammed tight in every corner. He had never seen so many people in it.

There was a murmur of excitement as he stepped out of the well of the court into the dock.

It could not be real.

It *was* real.

The room was large and lofty, with teak paneling, beautifully carved and figured, and a ceiling with Justice holding her scales immediately over the raised bench.

There were three magistrates, two men, and one woman. He knew them all, and it came as a shock to realize that two were on committees on which he also served.

They were "Justin" and "Leah" to each other. "Justin" and "George." "Justin" and "Arthur." Now they sat not as friends but in judgment upon him.

The public benches were so crowded that it would have been impossible to get another body in. The press box, where usually two young reporters sat, was crammed full; there were seven or eight, at least. But in the dock he seemed remote from all of them. Behind him were two policemen. In front of him another policeman. In front of the bench was the magistrates' clerk, and a young girl with a machine that was being tried out in Hodenham. Near them, by himself on a small bench, was Tomlinson, who looked up at him and smiled. The police lawyer, tall, melancholy-looking and balding, was with a plainclothes policeman.

The magistrates' clerk stood up.

"The accused is Mr. Justin Gray, sir."

That "Mr." was unusual—indicative of his feelings, his sympathies.

"Yes. And the charge?" The chairman of the magistrates was George Leather, owner of one of the larger local building firms.

"The charge, Your Worships, is that he, Justin Gray, did on the nineteenth of June in this year of grace, administer to one Mrs. Louise Pantanelli an injection of digitalin, knowing and intending that it would be fatal."

"So. Does the prisoner wish to say anything?"

"If I may, Your Worship, I would like to enter a plea of not guilty for the prisoner, whom I represent," said Tomlinson, "and to ask that evidence be heard."

"A plea of not guilty," the magistrate echoed. He glanced at his fellow magistrates and went on, "Yes." He peered down at the clerk. "Very well. Are the police represented? On a grave charge of this nature, they should be."

The police lawyer, whom Justin knew only slightly, stood up.

"Yes, sir, I represent the police in this instance. We would like to offer evidence of arrest and—"

"Shall we have the evidence of arrest first, please?"

"Very good, sir."

"If the officer concerned will take the stand. . . ."

The witness box was on the other side of the courtroom, and was approached from a different door, not from the well of the court. Eric Malleson appeared, very well-dressed, very solid-looking.

He took the oath, as he stood squarely to attention.

"Did you arrest the accused?" demanded George Leather, almost censoriously.

"I did, sir." Malleson sounded subdued.

"Give us details, please."

"Very good, sir. On the afternoon of Wednesday . . ."

Malleson told the story exactly as it had happened, in a clear, carrying voice.

"Thank you. You may stand down."

"If I may, Your Worship, I should like to ask for a remand in custody for eight days," the police lawyer said, standing up. "That will give time for us to conclude our inquiries."

Leather looked at Tomlinson.

"I don't think we need to inquire after today," said Tomlinson. "Have I the Court's permission to make a statement?"

He seemed so very sure of himself—unbelievably sure, almost laconic in his manner.

Leather darted a glance right, a glance left, and then said, "Proceed, Mr. Tomlinson, proceed."

"Thank you, sir. I do not think the police will question my statement that they have based their case—"

"Your Worship!" protested the police lawyer. "Surely it is for the *police* to state the basis of their case? Anything else is presumptuous!"

"Supposing we hear it, before deciding whether it is presumptuous or not," said Leather tartly.

He was being as well-disposed as he could be, Justin thought. But what on earth was Tomlinson going to say? What made him so confident?

"Thank you, sir." Tomlinson was completely self-assured. "The police have based their case on the testimony of witnesses who—"

"I really must protest," the police lawyer interrupted, almost excitedly.

"We *will* hear Mr. Tomlinson out," insisted Leather sharply. "This is a preliminary hearing only. The bench will decide what, and who, should be heard."

The lawyer sat down.

"The police have based their case on witnesses who saw the accused in certain places in which he denied being," went on Tomlinson. "On behalf of my client, I submit that these witnesses are mistaken and—"

"I really must . . ." began the police solicitor, half rising.

Leather and his fellow magistrates huddled together, and then Leather declared in a testy voice:

"Are the police witnesses available?"

"They are indeed, sir!"

"Then call them," ordered Leather.

"Very good, sir. The first witness is Miss Bertha Briggs."

Bertha gave evidence of seeing Justin talking to Micky Jones, and of seeing him leave the office at three-thirty on the day Mrs. Pantanelli died.

Peggy Nelson gave evidence of seeing Justin turning into Hillcrest.

The Carmichaels gave evidence of seeing Justin standing outside Mrs. Pantanelli's bedroom.

Micky Jones gave evidence of being paid by Justin to find the dead dogs and place them in the two doorways.

When they had all finished, the police lawyer said with dignity:

"On behalf of the police, sir, I submit that the evidence we have heard is more than enough to justify their request for a remand in custody, in the expectancy of committal for trial." He gave Tomlinson a long, triumphant stare, and sat down.

"Mr. Tomlinson," Leather said unhappily, "what have you to say?"

"I would like to call Mr. James Pantanelli," stated Tomlinson simply.

"Call Mr. Pantanelli," ordered Leather.

Who is he? Justin screamed silently. I've never heard of him! Pantanelli. *Pantanelli!*

A man appeared near the witness box and went slowly toward it. Every eye was turned on him, the courtroom was hushed. The man was tall. He was fair-haired. He was pleasantly good-looking. He wore a jacket in the casual style Justin usually wore. Across the courtroom, it seemed to Justin almost as if he were looking at himself.

He heard someone cry out, heard one or two subdued gasps.

He stared at the man in utter amazement.

Then he was seized by a sudden fierce excitement, and the hated tightness around his head. He began to shake violently. He knew that people were shouting, talking, holding him, but he was aware of very little else until there was the flame of brandy on his lips and in his throat. Slowly, slowly, his head cleared, and he was aware of two policemen, of Leather, of a gray-haired woman, all in front of him. His collar and tie were loose, his forehead wet. He was sitting back in a wooden chair, a policeman behind him keeping it upright.

"He's looking better," someone said.

"Justin, we can postpone this hearing if you're not well." This was Leather speaking.

Slowly, slowly, Justin remembered what had happened before his collapse, pictured the entry of the man who was so like him, recalled Tomlinson's voice as he had asked to call as witness Mr. James Pantanelli.

He, Justin, had never heard of a James Pantanelli.

Justin half rose from the chair and saw the stranger who looked almost like his twin in the witness box, tall and somehow aloof from the buzzing bedlam in the court. He was looking straight across at Justin, who now pulled himself to his feet, muttering:

"I'm all right. Don't worry about me, I'm all right."

Leather looked at him intently, then turned out of the dock. So did the others. The clerk of the court was calling for silence, the babble began to subside. The policeman behind Justin pushed the chair forward.

"Why don't you sit down, sir."

"Sir"—to a prisoner in the dock.

He sat down: shocked, unbelieving, bewildered, but quite calm. In the next few moments there appeared to be no one in the court except him and Pantanelli.

Why had he never heard of James Pantanelli?

Pantanelli was holding the Bible, taking the oath; he was somber of expression, and his eyes were narrowed. Tomlinson, behaving at first like a disinterested spectator, moved a little nearer to the witness and spoke in a clear, carrying voice.

"Mr. Pantanelli, I would like to state publicly in this court my appreciation of the fact that, once you were informed of the gravity of the situation in which Mr. Justin Gray had been placed, you agreed voluntarily to come to this court and to answer questions even though aware that some of the questions might put you at a disadvantage."

Pantanelli—*Pantanelli*—nodded distantly.

"My first question," went on Tomlinson, "is to ask whether you were any relation to the late Mrs. Louise Pantanelli, of Hilltop, here in Hodenham."

"Yes," answered James Pantanelli brusquely. "I am her son."

There was a gasp from a dozen people, but most were too breathlessly interested to cause any disturbance. Justin was oblivious of everything except the two men across the court. Pantanelli was full-face toward him and the likeness was unbelievable; it was as if he were looking into a mirror.

"Who was your father, Mr. Pantanelli?"

"Mario Pantanelli," answered the tall man, in the same clipped voice.

"Thank you. Are you aware that your father and mother lived here in Hodenham for over ten years, and your mother, after your father's death, for another ten years?"

"Yes, I am aware of it."

"Did you ever visit them during those years?"

"No."

"Will you please tell me why?" asked Tomlinson very quietly.

"I was estranged from them," answered James Pantanelli. "Before they came to live in Hodenham I had married against my father's wishes, and he had given me a substantial sum of money and washed his hands of me."

"What did you do?" asked Tomlinson.

"Your Worship . . ." the police lawyer began.

"Later," Leather shushed him. "Later."

"I settled in Rhodesia," said Pantanelli.

Rhodesia, thought Justin, and then with a sharp sense of shock: *Charlotte came from Rhodesia.* He clenched his hands tightly on his lap.

"And when did you return to England from Rhodesia?"

"A month ago," answered Pantanelli.

"Why did you return?"

"I had lost most of my money and possessions, due to the sanctions imposed by Britain, and I came to ask my mother for financial help."

It seemed as if everyone in the court drew in a sharp breath.

"Did she help you?" asked Tomlinson, almost casually.

"No," said Pantanelli, "but I don't think she understood me. She kept calling me 'Justin' and said I was looked after in her will." Now, Pantanelli looked across at Justin, and for the first time there was warmth and agitation in his voice. "I had known for years that I had a half brother, a son born to my mother while my father was away. He then worked for an engineering company and had been sent to Australia. The child was adopted by Mr. and Mrs. Gray of Hodenham, and as far as I know my father was never told."

"Yet *you* were!" Tomlinson asserted.

"I was told by my parents' servants, the Carmichaels," said Pantanelli. "They were upset by my father's disapproval of my marriage, and I think—" He broke off.

"I imagine that you think they wanted to give you a weapon, but you disdained the use of it," said Tomlinson in his warmest voice. "That was very creditable, Mr. Pantanelli. Let us come to more recent times. What followed your visit to your mother a month ago? Did you meet Justin Gray at that time?"

"No," answered Pantanelli. "But I met Maurice Mendelson, his cousin. My wife and I—"

His wife, thought Justin; Charlotte, his *wife.*

"—were walking to the station and he was driving from it. He stopped, thinking I was Justin. We had a drink, and I told him who I was."

"And what followed?" asked Tomlinson.

"I think I was so upset, I talked too much," said Pantanelli ruefully. "In fact, I know I did. Maurice said he thought he could help to make my mother understand, so I gave him my address. A few days later he came to see me, told me that only my half brother, Justin, could make her understand, but flatly refused to do so—because, said Maurice, any money I was given would make his inheritance less. And I'm afraid I believed this," Pantanelli added—and he looked away from Tomlinson to Justin.

Half brother flashed through Justin's mind.

He was Louise Pantanelli's son.

And as the realization burst into his consciousness he felt a great surge of darkness, like an enormous shadow, the onset of the symptoms of collapse; and as he felt his legs and arms and all his body begin to tremble, he seemed to shout within himself:

I mustn't faint, I must hold on.

And he clenched his fists and gritted his teeth while the courtroom seemed to sway and everybody in it began to go around and around.

Chapter 21

THE WISDOM OF
DR. CELLINI

Justin was aware of the policeman behind him, hands firm on his shoulders, aware that Leather was staring at him; and so was Pantanelli, so were all the people in court. Everywhere about him was stillness and silence.

He did not faint; and slowly the room and the people in it seemed to steady, and he sat quite still, his body tingling with nerves but completely under his control. Almost as if there had been no pause, Tomlinson asked another question.

"I see. Did you make any attempt to see Justin?"

"No."

"Why not?"

"If he was the man Maurice said, it obviously wouldn't be any use," answered Pantanelli. "But what I *did* do was talk it over with my wife, and we decided to find out for ourselves what kind of man he was. She arranged to meet Justin by pretending to look for a house, and they spent some time together."

"And what kind of man did she decide that Justin was?" demanded Tomlinson ironically.

"Your Worship," said the police lawyer in a sighing voice, "this is hearsay evidence, we really shouldn't—"

Leather looked at him; the whole court looked at him; and he subsided.

"My wife is here to speak for herself if you wish her to," said Pantanelli. There was a pause, but no comment or request, and he went on, "She found Justin extremely likable in one way, and utterly immovable in another. She thought it a waste of time trying to persuade him to do anything he didn't want to do. I think—I like to think," Pantanelli corrected, "that I would have gone to see Justin, but Maurice then convinced me that my mother was dying. He asked me first to meet him at his offices on the afternoon when she collapsed, and then persuaded me to go and visit her. I waited outside her room but didn't go in, for Maurice came out and told me she had collapsed. I came away," added Pantanelli simply. "As far as I was concerned, then, it was over. I wanted to leave England again, there was no point in staying. And Maurice made it possible by giving me a thousand pounds if I would leave at once. He said it would avoid scandal, and that he would find a way of getting the money back from Justin."

"Were any conditions imposed with the gift?" asked Tomlinson.

"Only that my wife and I had to leave at once. We were planning to fly out when you came to see us last night at the Outram Hotel."

"Where you were staying under your own name, and your wife wasn't known by the name she had given Justin."

"That's right," said James Pantanelli. "Of course, we guessed that there was *something* fishy going on, but I wanted that money so badly. Maurice must have gambled that we would be out of the country before there was any talk of murder, or of Justin being accused," he added grimly.

"Had you the slightest suspicion that murder was intended?" demanded Tomlinson.

"Absolutely none," answered Pantanelli.

"Your Worships," said Tomlinson, turning toward the bench, "before asking you to dismiss the charge against Justin Gray I would be grateful for your further indulgence"—he smiled at the police lawyer, who was now sitting up like a penitent before his priest—"to make one or two pertinent observations. I hope the police will consider certain possibilities—that Maurice Mendelson not only arranged for Mr. Pantanelli to be at Hilltop at the time when some individual, as yet unknown, gave her the fatal injection, but that the same Maurice Mendelson stole Mrs. Pantanelli's will. It may well be that the police will consider that out of his lifelong enmity toward Justin—"

"I think that's enough," interrupted Leather briskly. "Although I am sure the police will be interested in these observations." He inclined his head toward Tomlinson. "Meanwhile the Bench is glad to—the Bench unanimously dismisses the charge against Justin Gray."

He sat back in obvious satisfaction.

There was first a buzz of talk, then a sudden hubbub, as Justin climbed down from the dock and his half brother James crossed the well of the court toward him.

It was strange to stand together, shaking hands.

An hour later there was a crowd in Justin's flat: James, who was strangely tongue-tied, Justin, Dr. Cellini, Tomlinson, and Peggy, who was quite radiant. Cellini, standing with his back to the window, was speaking quietly.

"It was quite apparent that the witnesses weren't lying, and to me equally apparent that *you* weren't—so the witnesses must have seen not you but someone who was very like you. The first, Bertha Briggs, is very short-sighted. The second, Peggy Nelson, saw you, or thought she saw you, at a distance. The Carmichaels saw you, or thought they saw you, on a shadowy landing. Our obvious problem, then, was to find the man they really saw."

"Why didn't you tell me?" asked Justin, as quietly. "Why leave me to sweat it out?"

"Because we could not be sure we would find him. And but

for Mr. Tomlinson, we would not have done so. He called in a private detective who went to the hotel and soon learned that the woman you knew as Warwick was in fact Mrs. Pantanelli, and that her husband was not only your half brother but so like you that you might have been twins. It was then simply a matter of persuading the Pantanellis to postpone their flight. And they needed little persuasion.

"As for Micky Jones, well, Hugo Mendelson's a pretty good amateur actor. . . ."

Justin stared. "You mean it was *Hugo* who asked Jones to put those dogs on the doorstep? But *why?*"

Cellini stroked his mustache. "All part of the campaign to make you leave the business—a campaign that got a little out of hand," he added gravely. "Hugo seems to have been completely under Maurice's thumb. Justin, you will ask me why I did not prepare you for the revelations that were made in court. And some will ask why the police were not informed, for if they had been, the charge would most certainly have been withdrawn. And, indeed, I deliberated very deeply before deciding not to ask to see you or them last night after I talked to Hugo and Maurice. I came to the conclusion that the whole affair would be best aired fully, in public, so as to remove any last vestige of suspicion in anyone's mind. And I decided also that a public revelation of the truth about your parentage would be infinitely preferable to a private one, for this way it will be a nine-day wonder, the other way it would have been a subject for rumor and gossip for years. All the truth is now known, you have nothing more to face, only the facts to accept."

"Yes," Justin said dryly. "Yes, I see that. And it will—it will be easier." He looked at his half brother, almost unbelievingly, and gave a twisted smile. "I don't know whether to wish you'd come to see me or not. I might easily have suspected you were put up to pretend to be my"—there was a momentary pause—"my brother. As it is—" He broke off.

"Very difficult to know what to say," said Pantanelli, half smiling. "And harder for you than for me. I think the best way is for me to go off, as planned—they're holding seats on tonight's flight. Then when you're more used to the idea we can meet again. That . . . er . . . that's if you want another meeting with Charlotte."

"When I last saw her I hoped I'd see a great deal of her," said Justin ruefully. "I couldn't have made a very good impression."

"As a matter of fact you made a very big one," Pantanelli said. "And long before she actually cut and ran she hated the whole business."

"Why don't you leave the future to the future?" asked Cellini gently.

"Very wise," said Tomlinson.

"Yes," agreed Justin. "Yes, I suppose it's best. Er . . ." He stopped, suddenly feeling awkward and not knowing how to go on, then burst out, "Your money worries are over, anyhow, whatever our—our mother left has to be shared equally between us. I hope you won't—" He broke off.

Tomlinson murmured, "There are legal provisions to make sure James couldn't be disinherited, but it's much better like this. *Much* better."

James Pantanelli said gruffly, "That private eye has my address, Justin. Do keep in touch."

He gripped Justin's hand, then turned and strode away.

Justin went to the window and watched him walking toward the gate, then saw Charlotte appear for a moment by the side of a taxi. She looked up at the window and could not have failed to see Justin, who smiled and raised his hand.

She half raised hers before they disappeared.

"So it was Maurice who murdered Mrs. Pantanelli," said Peggy in a tight, high-pitched voice. "Not the others."

"Just Maurice," agreed Cellini. "The others knew nothing about it. I imagine that the police are questioning him now, and that he will confess to them, as he confessed to me, that he knew about the digitalin and that he gave the injection." He turned to Justin. "To start with, he simply wanted you driven out of the firm—that was why he told Hugo to see Micky Jones about those dogs. Why did Hugo disguise himself as you?" Cellini shrugged. "Who knows? Perhaps sheer love of intrigue, perhaps in case of any comeback. All pretty nasty, but so far, nothing technically against the law. It was when Maurice ran into James Pantanelli and discovered that you were Mrs. Pantanelli's son that the real trouble began."

"But the will—someone stole it from Freeman and Ross and put it in my flat," said Justin faintly. "Surely Maurice . . . ?"

Cellini nodded. "He had to find out who inherited the Pantanelli fortune—you or your half brother. If it was James, he was pretty confident, after his talk with him, that he could persuade him to invest a large portion in the business. When he found that James inherited nothing and that the entire fortune was left to you, something seemed to snap. All his resentment at not being able to get his hands on the old lady's property, all his hatred of you, suddenly grew out of all proportion, until, in this respect at least, he was no longer sane. Your startling resemblance to your half brother triggered off this amazing, crazy scheme for revenge."

"I can tell you another thing my private detective turned up, Justin," put in Tomlinson. "Maurice tried to get you out of your office on the afternoon of the murder. Bertha Briggs told us about a call from a man named Smethwick who wanted to meet you at a house in North Hodenham. There isn't such a man at that house, it was an obvious trick to get you out of the office at the crucial time. Luckily for him, though not for you, your half brother looked in to see him that afternoon. Maurice had told him to use the side entrance, which he did, but even so, Bertha saw him leave, and very naturally thought it was you. Hence her evidence. Well!" Tomlinson moved forward, hand outstretched, "I'll see you soon, Justin. Meanwhile, congratulations—and forgive me for tearing into you as I did. It wasn't until then that I felt absolutely sure of you. Whereas Manny here never had any doubts. Eh, Manny?"

Dr. Cellini simply smiled . . .

And shook hands . . .

And kissed Peggy on the cheek.

Justin stood by Peggy's side at the window, looking down as Dr. Cellini walked with Tomlinson toward the latter's car. Cellini did not pause or turn around, but raised his hand, to tell them that he knew they were watching.

"Justin," Peggy said, "he's so simple and good, I can hardly believe him."

Justin turned, stared, and then, to her astonishment, burst out laughing.

"He's too good to be true!" he said. "Too good to be true!"

He felt so incredibly different that he knew he would never have another relapse. He now knew *all* the truth, even the reason for Mrs. Pantanelli's affection for him, for her love. It was strange, but he would always think of his true mother as Mrs. Pantanelli, and of his foster mother with deep and lasting affection. And he had a brother. He was smiling because of that, and because he could understand and readily forgive Charlotte. And because Peggy's hand was creeping into his.

Three months later, Dr. Cellini was sitting in his living room, with the window closed against the autumn's chill, the gold caskets back from the Hodenham Museum, his wife, knitting, in a chair opposite him.

He was reading the *Evening News.*

There was a long report of the trial of Maurice Mendelson, who had been found guilty of the murder of Mrs. Pantanelli, and had been sentenced to life imprisonment. And there was an inset which said:

> *Mr. Justin Gray, a witness in the trial, is to turn the business of Mendelson and Gray into a limited company. Mr. James Pantanelli, who has recently returned to this country from Rhodesia, will be on the board. Mr. Hugo Mendelson and Mr. Alan Mendelson are no longer associated with the firm.*

"I suppose," said Dr. Cellini, over the newspaper, "we will soon have an invitation to the wedding. Tomlinson tells me that since the court hearing and his engagement to Peggy Nelson, Justin has been a different man."

"Not so good, you mean?" asked his wife.